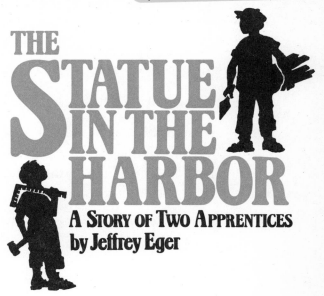

THE STATUE IN THE HARBOR

A STORY OF TWO APPRENTICES
by Jeffrey Eger

Silver Burdett Company
Morristown, New Jersey and Agincourt, Ontario

DEDICATED TO

*Sister Nelly in France, who taught
me my first words of French when
I was ten years old.*

And to Erik and Asa.

* * *

ACKNOWLEDGMENTS

We would like to thank the following individuals for their guidance
and helpful suggestions: Herbert Ershkowitz, Professor of
History, Temple University; Betty Grebey, Library Coordinator,
Downingtown Senior High School.

Cover Photograph © 1983 Peter B. Kaplan

Illustrations by Paula Goodman

Cover and interior design by Doug Bates

Joanne Fink, Project Editor

Suzanne Reynolds, Photo Research

* * *

Library of Congress Cataloging-in-Publication Data

Eger, Jeffrey.
 The statue in the harbor.

 Bibliography: p.
 Summary: Ten-year-old Philippe becomes apprenticed
as a coppersmith to his father in the Parisian foundry
where the Statue of Liberty is being constructed under
the direction of Frederic Auguste Bartholdi, and the
ensuing years shape the rest of his life.
 1. Statue of Liberty (New York, N.Y.) — Juvenile
fiction. 2. Bartholdi, Frederic Auguste, 1834–1904 —
Juvenile fiction. [1. Statue of Liberty (New York, N.Y.)
— Fiction. 2. Statues — Fiction. 3. Copperwork — Fiction.
4. Paris (France) — Fiction. 5. Bartholdi, Frederic
Auguste, 1834–1904 — Fiction] I. Title.

PZ7.E285St 1986   [Fic]   85-61511
ISBN 0-382-09146-9 (pbk.)
ISBN 0-382-09145-0 (lib. bdg.)

Published simultaneously in Canada by GLC/Silver Burdett Publishers

Manufactured in the United States of America

TABLE OF CONTENTS

INTRODUCED TO LIBERTY

Philippe Peden was just ten years old. More than anything, he loved to walk through the streets of Paris, smelling the fresh loaves of baked bread, listening to the singing calls of the vegetable sellers in the open-air market, and watching the horse-drawn carts and carriages moving slowly along the crowded streets and boulevards. Philippe felt alive and happy in this city full of color, smells, and movement.

Philippe no longer went to school like the children of the wealthy did. His father was a worker, and children of workers usually did not finish school. In time he would become an apprentice to his father, who worked as a coppersmith in the large metal foundry of Gaget, Gauthier and Co. at 25 rue de Chazelles. He looked forward to the day when his father would ask him to work. But in the meantime, he was satisfied and content to have the freedom to explore the narrow streets of his neighborhood.

Every day at lunchtime, Philippe's mother packed a food basket that Philippe carried to his father at work. She lined up all the things on the kitchen table and carefully put them into the basket, almost as if she were packing a gift. A bottle of red wine; a loaf of fresh, crusty warm bread; a thick piece of salami; some cheese that tickled your nose; and some green onions — all these were wrapped in a red checkered napkin and placed gently in the wicker basket with a lid.

"Now don't swing the basket, Philippe," his mother warned him with a little smile.

"Oui, Maman (*Yes, Mother*)," said Philippe. And he gave his mother a kiss on each cheek.

"Au revoir (*Good-bye*)," said Madame Peden (Mrs. Peden) as she wiped her hand on her long apron.

As soon as he reached the street, Philippe began skipping. It was a perfect spring day for skipping and even for running a little. Down the street and across the wide boulevard filled with black carriages and vegetable wagons, Philippe skipped, swinging the basket along the way. Then he took a shortcut through a narrow alley that led into a small courtyard, where he stopped to say "bonjour (*hello*)" to skinny Monsieur Pointier (Mr. Pointier) and his fat gray cat, Zizi.

"Here," Philippe said, breaking off the tip of the long loaf of bread in the basket. Zizi rubbed up against Philippe's leg, purred loudly, and sat down to eat the morsel of bread.

"Tomorrow I will put some apricot jam on the bread," Philippe told Zizi.

"Don't do that, boy," M. Pointier warned him. "Cats don't like sweet things the way you kids do. It would only make her ill. Now run along. Your father is probably hungry." Philippe waved goodbye and skipped down the alley. "And don't swing the basket," shouted M. Pointier.

When Philippe came out into the street again, he looked right, then left, and hopped on one foot across the cobblestones. "Seven hops today," he thought to himself as he arrived at the other side.

Right above him, in large letters, hung a huge sign that read Gaget, Gauthier and Company. Beneath the sign was an

Philippe took a short cut through a narrow alley that led into a small courtyard.

enormous iron gate. Philippe stood on his tiptoes and pulled the bell rope twice. While he waited, he kicked two stones across the street and pulled up his left sock. And then a big, deep, booming voice rang out. "Qui est la? (*Who is there?*)"

"Philippe Peden, monsieur. I have lunch for my papa."

An old watchman with a dirty blue beret and cracked black boots swung open the creaky gate. "Well, you only have to ring once. I have two ears, and they are both working. Your papa will be angry that you are late. Run along, boy. And be careful not to bump into anything sharp. You know where to find him."

"I know," said Philippe. "Down the courtyard, 'round the back, a left and another left." And with a wink he was gone, swinging the basket, whistling and skipping.

All around him, workmen were rushing, carrying boards and lifting gleaming sheets of copper the color of a bright new penny. The air was thick with plaster dust that made everything and everyone look like they were covered with a fine layer of snow. Wood chips and thin, curly wood shavings littered the ground. Small pieces of copper glittered among the scraps of wood. And the noise! Every corner of the immense workshop was filled with the sound of work: hammers pounding, grinders growling, chisels chipping, sandpaper scraping — just like an orchestra of workmen each playing a different tool. Shouts came from everywhere, echoing in the huge high ceiling of the workshop. It was exciting but very noisy. "How can anyone think with such noise?" thought Philippe. "It must be the loudest and dustiest place in all of Paris!"

But where was Papa? A heavy man with a bushy mustache tapped Philippe on the shoulder. He spoke at the top of his lungs. "Oh, it's you! You're Peden's son, aren't you? Got his lunch, do you?" And then the man yelled the loudest yell that Philippe had ever ever heard, "PEDEN!" For a moment the entire workshop quieted down. M. Peden looked up from his hammering and waved to Philippe to walk over to him. Philippe kissed his father on both cheeks and handed him the lunch basket. Someone gave a screechy whistle and shouted, "Lunchtime!" Then the only sound you could hear was that of all the workmen dropping their tools at the same time.

Philippe's papa opened the basket and noticed at once that the red checkered napkin was damp. He held it to his nose. "Have you been skipping again, Philippe?" Papa asked. "This napkin smells like spilled wine."

"Only one or two skips," said Philippe shyly.

"And who ate the end of my bread?" asked Papa, who seemed to be even more annoyed at that.

"I was attacked by Zizi, M. Pointier's cat," answered Philippe, his face very serious.

M. Peden roared with laughter, slapping his friend on the back. "Did you hear that, Dupont? Attacked by a cat! Are you sure it wasn't a tiger?" asked M. Peden, wiping away the tears of laughter.

"No, just Zizi," said Philippe. "He doesn't like sweet things, you know. They make him sick. He only likes bread without jam," Philippe concluded with a smile.

"Listen," Philippe's papa said to his son in a serious, low voice. "Don't you think that you are too old now to be playing with Zizi? Aren't you a little bored with skipping and bringing me lunch every day?"

"Oh no, Papa. I like to bring you lunch. I look forward to coming here every day," exclaimed Philippe.

"Then how would you like a pair of work boots? How would you like to work with me and Dupont and the other men who are building the Statue of Liberty?"

Philippe looked up at his father with wide eyes. For months

"You will be my apprentice. You will learn to be a master coppersmith."

he had been quietly waiting for him to ask that very question. But his mother had told him to be patient because Papa would know when the time was right.

"You mean, I will get a real pair of heavy work boots?" asked Philippe.

"Certainly, and heavy pants also. This is hard, dirty work," Papa replied.

"And I will work with the copper, just like you do?" asked Philippe excitedly.

"Sure, why not? You will be my apprentice. You will learn to be a master coppersmith," his father said with pride, rubbing his son's head affectionately.

"Oh, Papa," Philippe said, hugging his father, "I knew you would ask me. It has always been my secret dream to work with you and learn to be a coppersmith. Are you sure it will be all right with the other workers?" asked Philippe, a littie worried.

"Leave that to me," said Papa, pointing his big thumb at himself.

M. Peden finished his lunch quickly. He took a last swallow of wine from the bottle and pushed the cork in with his fist. "Now, let me introduce you to the important people here. You must always answer people politely. 'Oui, monsieur' or 'non, monsieur.' (*Yes, sir,* or *no, sir*) Remember, Philippe, you are a boy and they are men who deserve your respect. This is a different world than skipping and Zizi."

Philippe followed his father around the workshop, walking a few steps behind him. The boy was introduced to so many people that he could not remember all their names, and he had never shaken so many hands. He met M. Parent, the head carpenter; M. Beron, the head modeler; M. Simon, the sculptor's assistant; and M. Bergeret, the master of the metal and copperworkers. In addition, there were many plasterers, measurers, assistants, and even another boy who was an assistant (although Philippe had not met him yet). Finally Philippe was told to sit and wait to meet the chief engineer and the sculptor himself.

Philippe sat on a rough wooden worktable. He played with a hammer he had found on the table while he waited. Two men stood in front of him and spoke heatedly about something. The short one, named Eiffel, waved his hands in the air as if he were drawing an imaginary picture. The other one, who had a beard, shook his head and shrugged his shoulders. Finally they shook hands. Then M. Peden walked over to them and said he would like to introduce his son to them. They nodded. M. Peden gestured to Philippe to stand up and walk over.

"Gentlemen, may I present to you my son, Philippe Peden. If it is all right with you, I would like to have him work with me as my apprentice. Philippe, this is M. Frédéric Auguste Bartholdi, the great sculptor who designed and created the statue. And this is M. Gustave Eiffel, the engineer who has come up with a clever way to make the statue stand forever." M. Peden gave Philippe a little push, whispered something in his ear and Philippe held out his hand.

"I am honored to meet you Monsieur Bartholdi, Monsieur Eiffel," Philippe said in a clear voice.

"The workshop may look a little disorganized and cluttered right now, but in two or three weeks you'll know everyone by name and where everything is placed," responded M. Bartholdi.

"He's right, you know, young man," said M. Eiffel. "He is hardly ever wrong."

M. Eiffel gave Bartholdi a playful pat on the back. Bartholdi laughed and said, "He's right, you know. He is hardly ever wrong."

Bartholdi turned to Philippe and said, "Philippe, come with me. I would like to show you something of great interest." Bartholdi excused himself and walked with Philippe to the far side of the workshop. In a neat, clean corner where M. Bartholdi worked, there stood a table on which was placed a mysterious object covered by a white cloth. Bartholdi walked over to the table and slowly pulled a string. The cloth rose to reveal a beautiful statue about 4 feet tall. It was made of clay. "Voilà, the Statue of Liberty!" Bartholdi said, raising his arm in a gesture like that of the statue. In the pale, soft light the statue glowed as if it were lit from the inside.

"There she is — my daughter. She is not really my daughter, but I like to think that she is," Bartholdi confided to Philippe in a whispering voice.

Philippe also whispered, although he didn't know why, "She is so small. I thought she was bigger than the houses. Why do you need all these men to help you build something so small?"

Bartholdi smiled and spoke, "Even the biggest ideas must begin with the smallest thoughts. A grown man starts life as a baby; a palace of a king begins with a single brick or stone. This statue is only 4 feet tall. And yet it started from the tip of my pencil, which is even smaller. And the idea of its shape comes from the imagination, which we can't even see! But when your work is finished, the statue will rise high above the rooftops — over 150 feet high, and even higher when it is on its pedestal."

Just then a voice called, "Monsieur Bartholdi, can you come here? We want you to check this detail." And Bartholdi slowly lowered the cloth over the statue, making it look mysterious once again.

Philippe turned to the sculptor and said, "I like your imagination, Monsieur Bartholdi. I can picture the statue very well."

As Philippe turned, he looked at the workshop with new eyes. All the men seemed to be staring at him. Behind them, large pieces and sections of the statue were being worked

Inside the large workshop of the Gaget, Gauthier and Company foundry. The workers have been asked to stop work and hold still for the photographer.

on. Philippe could clearly see what Bartholdi meant. For a moment, everything seemed quiet and still, as if it were frozen in time. Then a whistle blew and the sound of the hammers, saws, and chisels filled the air. Men began to work and talk, first slowly and then quicker and quicker. The noise grew louder. Philippe stood there, amazed.

"Hey, are you Philippe?" Someone was tapping Philippe on the shoulder.

"Hello, anyone home? Are you Philippe?" It was a boy, a little taller and a bit older than Philippe.

"Yes, I'm Philippe. Who are you?"

"Jean Garcelon is my name. I'm an assistant here. I work in the carpentry shop."

"How long have you been working here?" asked Philippe.

"Oh, about a year and a half. You must be someone special. M. Bartholdi is so busy he never has time to speak to new workers."

"No, I'm just a regular kid. How old are you, Jean?"

"Thirteen. But I look younger, right?"

"I'm ten. This looks like hard work. How can you stand the noise?" asked Philippe.

"After a while you don't even notice it. You just have to speak loudly here," Jean shouted.

"Do you mind if I watch you work?" asked Philippe.

"Why not," replied Jean. "Let's go."

Jean returned to his job, handing blocks of wood to a carpenter, who fitted them into a large puzzlelike box. Then Jean would pound the block from one side while the carpenter knocked all the blocks down from the top. One after the other the blocks fell into place. "It looks simple enough," Philippe thought to himself.

As he walked through the workshop, he noticed the men working at different jobs. Some workers were covered in white dust as they put plaster on wooden forms. Farther on, two men were sitting on a scaffold, taking measurements of what looked like an arm. Nearby, another worker, a modeler, was scraping off small ridges of what seemed to be part of the statue's dress.

"Well, Philippe, what do you think?" asked his father, wiping his forehead with his dirty shirt sleeve.

"I never realized how many different kinds of work were needed just to make one statue," Philippe said, amazed.

"Not every statue needs this many workers. But this is a very special statue, the biggest in the world. And M. Bartholdi has had to design it in such a way that it can be shipped to

America by boat. You will understand in time," said Papa. "Now let me tell you the names of the different tools we use in copper work. You see, every craft has its own set of tools. Tools of the trade, they are called. What is good for wood is not strong enough for metal. And the men who work in plaster — well, they use tools that carpenters and coppersmiths could never use. Don't worry, though, in time it will all become clear to you."

Philippe looked up at his father. It felt good to be here. He was glad his father had asked him to be an apprentice. Maybe someday he would be the best coppersmith in Paris. As M. Bartholdi had said, "Everything big starts from a small beginning."

Monsieur Bartholdi (second from right) explains to a visitor how the wooden strips are placed and hammered onto the left arm.

CONSTRUCTING LIBERTY

The job of learning any new task is never easy. There were some days when Philippe thought he already knew as much as his father and the other coppersmiths who had been working for years. Then there were other days when he made so many mistakes and foolish decisions that he felt like giving up.

"Philippe, you have been working here for five months, now," said M. Bergeret one afternoon right after lunch. "I've been watching you closely. Although you are young, you have a very good head and you are able to figure out things quickly. What is more important, though, is that you seem to have the spirit that is needed to be an apprentice. In our coppersmith profession, as in any other, if you are bored with your work and do not feel challenged by it, all work will feel heavy. The reward is the work itself, to do it excellently."

"Thank you, Monsieur Bergeret, for the compliment," said Philippe, blushing a little. "I don't think I deserve it. This morning I made some silly mistakes and brought you the wrong tools three times. It is just that there are so many different names for hammers, mallets, and anvils. I think there must be more than seventy-five different kinds and shapes of hammers that we use on the copper," explained Philippe.

*S*ome *of the many tools used by Philippe, his father, and the other coppersmiths.*
The serpe *is on the far right in the top row, and the* bible *is at the very bottom.*

"If it is so confusing, then perhaps you should make a chart with the names and pictures of all of them. Then you would remember," suggested M. Bergeret. "Don't give up. We're all counting on you."

Philippe smiled. He felt better. It was always good to hear someone else tell you that you were doing a fine job. Especially when it was the master coppersmith himself.

That afternoon after work, Jean, the carpenter's assistant, and Philippe walked through the cobbled streets of Paris. They were two young boys dressed like men, discovering how their Paris looked after a hard day's work.

"Did you have a difficult time remembering all the names of the tools when you started, Jean?" asked Philippe.

"I'll say," said Jean. "It took me half a year at least, I think. And then once you learn the names, you have to learn how each tool is used. Being an assistant carpenter might look simple, but when you have to do it, that is quite different."

"I know what you mean, Jean. A lot is expected of us. We are in a man's world, but I still feel like a boy," said Philippe.

"I would have liked to go to school for a few more years, but my father told me that learning a trade, his trade, was the proper thing to do," Jean remarked resentfully. "I like it, don't get me wrong. It's only that I didn't have any choice."

"Not me," said Philippe. "I was bored doing nothing. I was waiting for the day when my father would ask me to join him in metalwork. Hey, do you want to visit a friend of mine who lives around here?" asked Philippe.

"Sure," said Jean. "But let's make it fast. My mother will be looking for me for dinner."

They crossed the street and ran into an alley. Jean was a few feet behind Philippe. It was one of Philippe's favorite places.

"Here, Zizi," he called. "Here, Zizi. Nice cat. Nice cat."

M. Pointier walked out of his shop and greeted Philippe. "I haven't seen you in months, Philippe," said the man. "I was wondering what had happened to you."

"I have been working, Monsieur Pointier. I am an apprentice coppersmith," remarked Philippe proudly.

"Over there on the rue de Chazelles?" asked M. Pointier. Philippe nodded. "Isn't that where they are building some kind of tremendous statue?" asked M. Pointier, spreading his arms wide to show how big the statue was.

"That's the place," said Philippe. "This is my friend, Jean. He is an assistant carpenter. Jean, this is M. Pointier, and this is his cat Zizi," said Philippe, making all the proper introductions.

"I have a cat named Lucy," said Jean, "and her favorite food is orange marmalade."

M. Pointier seemed surprised. "Orange marmalade? But cats don't like sweets…"

M. Pointier seemed surprised. His eyebrows rose as he exclaimed, "Orange marmalade? But cats don't like sweets..."

Jean smiled and nodded.

"A bientôt (*See you soon*)," said Philippe, waving to M. Pointier.

"I've got to run home," said Jean. "See you tomorrow."

Philippe arrived home just as his family was sitting down for supper. He quickly washed his hands and quietly took his seat. The other members of the family were already at the table. His father gave him a hard look; then he said grace. "Thank you for this bread and food. Amen." Philippe's mother served the steaming potato soup from the tureen.

"Where were you?" asked Babette, Philippe's younger sister. "You were late," she said in a grown-up voice, as if she were imitating her mother.

"With Jean. We visited M. Pointier and Zizi," said Philippe.

"You know when dinner is served, Philippe. You were late," said his father.

"It's all right, Papa," said Philippe's mother calmly. "Sometimes a boy needs a little free time even if he does do a man's work," she continued, smiling at her son.

"You're right, Maman," said Philippe's father, changing his angry tone. "He is really a very good worker. M. Bergeret told me he is very satisfied with Philippe. He has only good things to say about him," M. Peden said proudly.

Philippe smiled and said, "Papa, do you think that after dinner, you could help me with the names and shapes of the different tools we use? I want to make a chart, so I won't forget," said Philippe.

"Bien sûr (*Of course*)," said Papa. "But let's first finish this tasty soup your mother and sister have made."

After supper, under the gaslight, Philippe spread out a large piece of paper while his father sharpened two pencils. They sat down side by side at the table. "First let me draw the ones I remember," said Philippe. He drew seven different hammers.

"Do you know their names?" asked Papa.

Philippe pointed to each as he named them. "This is an embossing hammer, and this one is a cross pein. Here is a double cross pein." And he continued naming all seven.

"What about the other tools, Philippe?" Papa asked.

"Oh, there are many anvils, like the ball anvil, the stake anvil, and the bench anvil," said Philippe, sketching the shapes quickly.

"Excellent," said Papa. "This boy *has* learned something, Maman."

"Then there are the wooden mallets, and the rammers, and levers," said Philippe.

"Oh, the serpe. How could I forget that? It looks like a serpent," added Philippe.

"...And the one that looks like a book?" asked Papa, knowing that Philippe would have the answer.

"The bible," smiled Philippe. "That's because it looks like a Bible, hinged to fold and bend the copper sheets in straight lines."

"Fantastique!" said Papa, giving his son a kiss on the forehead. "You are teaching me," Papa said to Philippe, smiling at his son. And then Papa added many more tools to the chart, drawing them on the paper and explaining the use of each one.

"I shall bring this to work tomorrow," announced Philippe. "Thank you, Papa." And he gave his father and mother a good-night kiss and went off to bed.

The following weeks were busy ones at the workshop. Now that Philippe felt more self-confident about his work, he opened his eyes to all the different activities going on around him. At first it seemed that all the workers were working under the same roof but that each one was occupied with his own craft. But then Philippe began to understand the connection between one craft and another. Slowly, in his mind, he began to see the whole complex picture. He could tell when the carpenters were using saws and when they were hammering light boards together. His ear could detect the wet slurping sound of spreading plaster on wood. And, of course, he knew all the intricate sounds of the copper-working area even better. What seemed like noise months ago now had the rhythm of a kind of music.

When Philippe started working in the spring of 1880, the arm and the torch as well as the head of the statue had already been completed. The arm with its torch had been finished four years earlier, in 1876, and was shown at the Philadelphia Centennial Exposition, marking one hundred years of American independence. Millions of people had seen it at the fair. Many even paid ten cents to walk up the stairs to the top of the torch to have their pictures taken and get a bird's-eye view of the immense fairgrounds.

The head was completed next and was exhibited in a park during the Paris Exposition of 1878. It was the major attraction of the exposition. There, as in Philadelphia, visitors could walk up a flight of stairs to the top. Both exhibits had been popular attractions because people could not believe the huge size that the statue would be when it was finished. In fact, many newspapers made fun of the head and torch, saying that the sculptor should have started with the feet and then slowly worked up. But M. Bartholdi knew best. He chose the arm, the torch, and the head because, in a sense, they were symbols of what was to become the entire colossal statue.

Building a statue that stands 151 feet tall and is able to

The torch and the arm were first shown in Philadelphia in 1876.

Frédéric Auguste Bartholdi, the sculptor of the Statue of Liberty.

The head was exhibited in Paris in 1878.

withstand hurricane-force winds blowing at 140 miles an hour is no simple matter. It takes great planning and calculating. In the end, if everything goes well and according to plan, the end result — the statue — should look as if it were simple to build. Never before in history had such a huge statue been built.

This is what Philippe learned by asking many questions: Years before the work began in the workshop, the sculptor, Frédéric Auguste Bartholdi, thought and thought about a monumental statue. What should it look like? What was it to represent, and who was it to honor? These are the questions every sculptor or artist must ask before the idea for the design comes. Then the idea came to Bartholdi: The statue was to honor George Washington and the Marquis de Lafayette (a young French general who fought for liberty alongside Washington in the American Revolution). The idea was also to commemorate the help that France once had given America (then a colony of England) in gaining independence.

To design something as big as the Statue of Liberty, it was necessary to know a little about the place where the monument would eventually be placed. Since this statue was to be a gift from the French people to the Americans, it would stand on American soil. So Bartholdi went to America in 1871. He wanted to know two things: where such a statue would stand, and if the Americans liked his basic idea of a huge statue dedicated to liberty. For nearly two weeks he sailed across the Atlantic on a steamship. As soon as he arrived in New York harbor on an early June morning, he knew in his heart that this would be a wonderful place to erect a statue. But where? He saw a small island, Bedloe's Island, with its old abandoned fort. Right then and there, Bartholdi was positive that the island was a perfect site for an enormous statue. All around it was water and sky. Ships arriving in America would immediately be welcomed by the statue in the harbor. Bartholdi remembered this place as he continued his journey by train across America. As he trav-

eled, he was amazed at the gigantic size of the country —
the rivers, the Great Plains, the Rocky Mountains, the giant
Sequoias, the Pacific Ocean, and more. By the time he
returned to New York City, he had a suitcase full of sketch-
books, watercolors, and diaries. He realized that a statue
that honored the greatest land of liberty needed to be the
greatest statue ever created.

Bartholdi sailed back to France. He was brimming over with
new ideas. During the next three and a half years, he built
many clay models and made numerous sketches of his
ideas. He was a patient man who knew that anything worth
doing is worth doing well, with all one's heart and ability. He
asked his mother to be the model for the statue's face. She
had a strong face with sharp, beautiful features. Such a face,
thought Bartholdi, was exactly what was needed for so large
a sculpture.

Then he found another woman to be the model for the body
of the statue. Her name was Jeanne-Emilie Baheux de
Puysieux and she was a dressmaker's assistant. She had
the perfect appearance for the liberty statue: graceful
arms, good posture, a lovely neck, and beautiful legs. Later,
Bartholdi married her.

When Bartholdi had finished his design, he asked some
important French citizens to come view his work. The
group came to his studio to consider the statue. They all
agreed that it would be fitting for the people of France to
give the statue to the people of America. The Americans
would do their part by providing the pedestal upon which
the statue would stand. The model that the group saw was
the same one that Philippe saw in the workshop.

Money was raised all over France. Schoolchildren and small
towns sent in funds. A national lottery with many prizes was
organized, and more money was raised from the sale of
lottery tickets. Special musical events were held and the
proceeds went toward the construction of the statue. When
all the money had been raised, work began in full swing.

Bartholdi knew from the very beginning that the conventional methods of building would not work well for such an unconventional statue. He needed a material that would be light yet strong, solid yet flexible, and easy to bend and shape. But, perhaps greatest of all, he needed a material that was not too heavy or bulky and would be easy to transport across the Atlantic Ocean in crates by ship. He studied the problem and came up with a clever solution: *repoussé,* or hammered, copper. Copper had all the advantages and none of the disadvantages of bronze or other metals used in statue building. And it could be worked in pieces, which allowed many parts of the sculpture to be created at the same time by teams of carpenters, modelers, plasterers, and metal-workers. The only question that still had to be resolved was how the statue would stand.

such as?

Most statues are sturdy enough and thick enough to provide their own support. But copper sheets about the thickness of a silver dollar, or one-eighth of an inch, would blow away in the first wind storm. So Bartholdi, who was only the artist and sculptor, had to ask someone to help figure out how his liberty statue would stand. Gustave Eiffel was chosen for

*G*ustave Eiffel, the engineer who designed the skeleton for the statue and later designed the famous Eiffel Tower.

the job. Eiffel was an engineer who specialized in light-weight iron structures like railroad bridges, which could bear a great deal of stress.

After months of testing and figuring, Eiffel arrived at a solution: the thin skin of the statue would be supported by a system of iron bands, braces, and girders. It would look like a skeleton, much like the skeleton of a person. It could be erected anywhere, quickly and easily. And what is most important: it would be sturdy beyond belief. With this major problem solved, work on the statue began with gusto!

Bartholdi realized that you could not build the full-size statue immediately. It would be impossible to control the proportions. So, he enlarged his 4-foot clay model to a plaster model a little larger than 9 feet, or about one-sixteenth scale (sixteen times smaller than the final statue). At that size he had to adjust certain features of the way the robe appeared and the way the face looked. Then, with the help of the plasterers in the workshop, he enlarged the model four times to one-quarter size (or four times smaller than the final statue). Now it was about 37 feet tall. It was enormous. The carpenters raised the roof of the workshop so that the model would fit standing up. And then for the final step, the statue was enlarged four times again to actual size — the size in which it would be made in copper.

Now, that sounds simple, but it was not so at all. It was the last stage that had taken one hundred workers five years to achieve.

First each part of the statue had to be divided into sections. And each section had about nine thousand check points on it. There were more than three hundred sections of the statue and no two were similar.

The sections were made in horizontal levels, starting with the feet and the base. The next level included the area around the ankle. The next, covered the area right below the knee, and so on, all the way up. Each section was measured

A t work on the wooden molds. The coppersmiths begin to shape the copper according to the wooden molds.

with large compasses, lead wires called plumb lines, and rulers.

Before it was made in copper, each section went through many intermediate steps. First, a scale drawing was made and placed on the floor. Then a rough wooden form was constructed on the drawing. On that form, M. Parent and his team of carpenters cut and nailed thin strips of wood onto a wooden frame. The frame with the thin strips was then covered with a layer of plaster.

Then M. Beron and his team of modelers made corrections in the plaster, checking and double-checking every fold and every line.

Then a second form was constructed. It was covered with very fine lathework (long, thin wooden boards) and was made to conform to the outer skin of the plaster. This was the mold on which the copper sheets would be placed.

Then it was finally time for the metalworkers to begin. M. Bergeret, M. Peden, Philippe, and all the other coppersmiths would use the different large hammers, levers, and mallets to make the copper take on the form of the mold. A thin sheet of lead (which is very easy to press) was used as a kind of mold to help them with the small, intricate details. Sometimes they would have to heat the copper to shape it. Once they finished, the copper section was fitted with iron braces and straps on the inside to make the section rigid and sturdy. This is why the method is called repoussé, or hammered, copper — because the copper is pushed and hammered out from the inside to fit the wooden form.

After the coppersmiths finished a section, it was checked against the model. Then M. Eiffel and his team would be ready to place it on the iron skeleton that they had constructed in the courtyard.

It was indeed a complicated process. It took Philippe nearly ten months before he could understand every detail of it. He was most knowledgeable about the copper and metalwork, naturally. Every day was a challenge because each section of the statue was different from all the rest. Every bit of work was done by hand, with muscles and sweat.

Philippe had gained a reputation for being the best of the coppersmiths when it came to small details. His hands were small and he could work in spaces that the grown men could not reach with their large fingers. When they needed him, they would call him by his nickname, *Le Souris* (The Mouse), because he alone could get into places where no one else could fit. Philippe liked the name Le Souris. Even M. Bartholdi called him this. It was a name he accepted with pride!

CREATING LIBERTY

It was hard for Philippe to believe he had been an apprentice for a whole year. To his father, he was growing up in a man's world. He had become stronger and leaner from lifting heavy copper sheets and swinging hammers for ten hours a day. To his father, Philippe was a young man of eleven, but to his mother, Philippe was still a boy.

"Maman, I want to be an apprentice, too, and work with Papa when I am a little older," said Babette, Philippe's younger sister.

"How can you, Babette?" asked Mme. Peden. "You are a girl, and girls don't work with copper in workshops."

"But it isn't fair," Babette pouted. "I don't want to be a cook or a shop girl. I want to do the things Philippe does."

"I'm sorry, dear, but it just isn't done," explained Mme. Peden.

"Girls are not stupid. They just don't get the chance that boys do," argued Babette.

"Maybe someday they will. But for now, they must learn to do what women do," Mme. Peden said sympathetically.

"Now, will you help me with dinner? I have made Philippe's favorite meal: lamb stew and for dessert — apple tart. He has been an apprentice for one year. It is an important day."

"Maman, it isn't fair," complained Babette.

During dinner Babette did not speak. She had a long, grumpy face. She pushed her stew from one side of the plate to the other.

"Babette, why aren't you eating? This is Philippe's favorite meal. We are celebrating his first year as an apprentice." said M. Peden.

Philippe excused himself from the table and ran to his room. He returned with a small wrapped box. "Here, Babette, this is for you. I bought it with my own money," Philippe said, placing the gift in front of her.

Babette looked at the box and tried to smile. She opened the wrapping and found a little painted box inside. Slowly she opened the lid of the box and a ballerina began to dance to the sounds of a delightful piece of music.

"Isn't that lovely," her mother remarked. "That's very sweet of you, Philippe," she added.

"I knew Babette would like it," said Philippe, blushing.

"It is very pretty, Philippe," Babette said as she held the delicate gift in her hand. "Thank you, Philippe. It is not even Christmas or my birthday."

"It is just because you are my sister," said Philippe, smiling.

"Now let's eat," said Papa. "This wonderful meal is getting cold!"

There were more changes at the workshop. For the last week, workers had been clearing an area in the courtyard. Now a platform had been laid, a strong, heavy concrete platform. And on top of that were several layers of brick, Jean and Philippe ate their lunch as they walked around the flat space.

"I heard that M. Eiffel has finished his plans and is ready to begin erecting the iron skeleton," said Jean.

"Here, in the middle of the courtyard?" asked Philippe.

"Yes, and it will rise above the rooftops of the houses!" Jean added.

"So now I understand why we have been preparing the iron braces on the back of the copper sheets," said Philippe. "The time has come for the statue to rise!"

"Not so fast!" Jean remarked. "It is going to take them most of the summer and the fall just to put together the skeleton."

Slowly, week by week, the iron skeleton rose. It was made of four wrought iron posts, which were themselves made of many strong iron plates riveted together. People on the street could not understand what this strange structure was meant to be.

"It looks more like an oil derrick than a statue," said one man, leaning out of his carriage as he rode past.

"It is a metal monster from a Jules Verne book," said a frightened vegetable seller, sitting next to her produce stand.

"How can anything so ugly ever become something beautiful," added a well-dressed woman with a parasol and a poodle.

On into the summer, the ironworkers labored. The skeleton grew, but, it seemed, at a snail's pace. Eiffel's plan took into account many invisible problems that he knew could topple the statue if solutions were not found before the final construction. The four main posts were only the principal supports. In addition, a system of smaller iron braces and bars would be needed so that the statue's copper skin could be attached and secured. Eiffel's plan was to fasten the copper sheets to the flexible light braces and bars, rather

The lightweight structure which will support the statue begins to rise in the courtyard of the foundry.

than to the rigid central posts. Then, in a wind storm the structure would move slightly, like a spring. If it were not so flexible, it would snap like a pencil under pressure. But there was another reason why the skeleton was designed the way it was. It had to do with the weather, oddly enough. But Philippe was not to discover this for some time.

30

It was autumn. The trees near the courtyard were beginning to lose their leaves. The statue's skeleton was only half finished. Inside the workshop, more sheets of copper were being transformed and hammered and pressed into the wooden forms. The work had taken on a peculiar rhythm of a slow march. Measurers went first, then carpenters; plasterers followed; and then modelers. The work was interconnected, with each laborer playing a part in turn. Then the measurers returned to check proportions, the carpenters returned followed by the copper workers and the ironworkers. To someone who did not understand the process it would appear that things were being done several times. But to Philippe and the other workers, who realized how difficult the work was, it was all clear. Handwork like this demanded concentration and for that reason, while it was never boring, it was always exhausting. "Details," lectured Bartholdi to his workers, "are the key to the success of this statue."

From time to time, curious visitors wandered in off the street. Just by word of mouth, the statue had become quite a tourist attraction. As it became more visible, even more people came to marvel at its immense size. Usually M. Beron, Bartholdi's assistant, would talk about the statue and answer questions the tourists would ask. But sometimes on his lunch break, Philippe would answer questions as well. He liked to speak with the visitors. It made him feel important.

"We use many different tools in copper work, over seventy-five different hammers!" said Philippe to a group of schoolchildren and their teacher, who had just come through the gate of the Gaget and Gauthier workshop. "Every person has a job to do; each one is an expert craftsman. I am just an apprentice. M. Eiffel, the engineer, supervises the skeleton framework; and the sculptor himself, Frédéric Auguste Bartholdi, oversees every step of the production."

One day after Philippe had finished talking to a group,

M. Bartholdi happened to walk by. He had heard how well Philippe handled the group. Bartholdi interrupted and said to the group, "I would like to point out that this boy, Philippe Peden, is the youngest and most diligent worker here. He is only an apprentice but he works like a master!"

After the crowd left, Bartholdi turned to Philippe and said, "You know, what I just said was true, Philippe."

"But, sir, I still have so much to learn," said Philippe shyly.

"I have kept my eye on you. I believe you will go far because you have the desire to be the best coppersmith in France. You love your work. That is the difference between someone who does his job because it is a job and someone who does it because he sees it as his life." Bartholdi looked at Philippe and smiled at the boy, who was blushing, "How would you like to come to supper? My wife and I have no children and we would like it very much if you would join us for supper this week. Let's say Wednesday. My studio is part of the house, so I could show you my other sculptures and design studies of the projects on which I am working."

"I would love that, Monsieur Bartholdi," said Philippe, gleaming. "I shall ask my father for his permission."

When Philippe left his home that Wednesday evening to go to the Bartholdi's for dinner, he was dressed in his best Sunday clothes. Being dressed up made him feel grown up. As he arrived at the sculptor's studio, his heart was beating quickly.

Philippe had never seen so many sculptures in his life. He had never been to a museum, so this was the first time he had ever looked at real art. Oh, once he saw a painter in the street, painting a picture of a church. But this was altogether different. From the top to the bottom of the cluttered, high-ceilinged room, there were small clay models, busts of famous heroes, and models of the liberty statue's hand. All these filled shelves and perched on top of cabinets. On the top of a bookcase there was a model in plaster of *The*

"We use many different tools in copper work, over seventy-five different hammers!" said Philippe to a group of school children and their teacher.

Lion of Belfort, which Bartholdi had just completed for the town of Belfort in his native Alsace. The actual sculpture, made of stone and set into a mountainside in the town, was enormous, but the model was only about 2 feet long. Philippe walked slowly through the studio, examining each piece. He came to one sculpture, which was under a large, wet towel.

"What is this one?" Philippe asked inquisitively.

"I am working on that one at the moment," said Bartholdi. He carefully removed the towel and there stood a beautiful clay model of a man with his arm outstretched.

"Who is that?" asked Philippe.

"That is Rouget de Lisle, the composer of the "Marseillaise," our national anthem. See the musical notes on the paper at his feet?" said Bartholdi.

*B*artholdi's studio was filled with models of the many different sculptures he had designed. Many of his colossal ideas started here.

"But this won't be as large as the Statue of Liberty, will it, Monsieur Bartholdi?"

"No, no, not at all, Philippe. This will be much smaller. It will be about 9 feet tall and stand in a town square where the composer was born."

"Its arm is extended like that of the Liberty," observed Philippe.

"So it is, similar. You have a good eye," said Bartholdi. "Some statues are better in smaller size and some, like the Liberty, should be made huge."

"But how can you tell when to make them huge?" asked Philippe.

"First of all," Bartholdi explained, "a colossal statue must represent a big idea: not just a man on a horse or a national hero, but an idea that touches the heart and makes us feel something deeply. It must not be enormous just because the sculptor feels it would be nice to make it large. Making a sculpture as big as the Liberty is a great responsibility — not merely because of the cost in money or in the time of many workers, but because people will see it for as long as it stands."

"When the visitors come around to see the statue in the workshop they just cannot believe their eyes," observed Philippe.

"Yes, but they are reacting to the size alone and not to what it means," Bartholdi continued. "When they view it finished surrounded by water and sky in New York harbor in the New World, it will not only be a giantess; it will have meaning as well. The place where it stands will play an important role. Then and only then will it touch people the way I have envisioned.

Philippe looked around the studio again. "So many sculptures!" he thought. "Each one a different idea." He turned back to the sculptor and spoke, "How can you have so many ideas at the same time, one after the next? I am confused when I must think of only two things at once!"

Bartholdi laughed. "I was exactly like that when I was eleven, Philippe. It is called self-discipline. You teach yourself as you get older. Open your eyes, your ears. Develop your senses. Use your imagination, and focus on what you want to do. The rest will come by itself, rolling in at your feet."

"It sounds easy, Monsieur Bartholdi. But I know from my work as an apprentice, there is nothing easy about it," said Philippe.

"Frédéric, supper is ready," It was Jeanne-Emilie, Bartholdi's young wife.

"Let's continue this conversation at supper, Philippe. Even people who use their imagination all day get hungry at night."

Philippe had never eaten in such a fancy dining room, nor had he ever had a meal served to him by a servant. Sometimes when he walked past a café or restaurant he would see people enjoying a meal, but the children of workers just didn't have such opportunities!

There were only three people at the large table: M. Bartholdi at the head, Jeanne-Emilie to his right, and Philippe, who sat in the guest's seat to the left. A white lace cloth covered a pink undercloth. A silver candlelabra with six flickering candles sat in the center of the long table. The rest of the room was lit by gaslight, which produced an eerie pale light.

Philippe tucked his napkin under his chin. Mme. Bartholdi placed her napkin on her lap. M. Bartholdi looked at Philippe and then at his wife. What should he do? He had always placed his napkin on his lap, as most well-to-do Parisians did. But if he did so now, Philippe would feel out of place, and a host must never make his guest feel out of place. So Bartholdi placed his napkin under his chin. His wife looked at him and smiled.

"Soupe d'oignon," announced the serving woman as she placed the plates of soup in front of Philippe and his two hosts. The steaming soup smelled delicious. Philippe looked at the side of his plate. Four spoons! He had never seen four spoons. He didn't know which to choose. At home, everyone got one spoon and that was it! He waited discreetly for M. Bartholdi to choose the proper spoon. It was the largest.

"How could I ever fit that giant spoon in my mouth," Philippe thought to himself. He watched Mme. Bartholdi hold the spoon delicately between her thumb and next two fingers. She put the spoon in the soup gently and filled it half-way. Then she placed it sideways to her lips and sipped from it very quietly. "So that's the way it's done," thought Philippe, realizing that it was not that difficult.

Philippe looked at the side of his plate. Four spoons! He had never seen four spoons at one place setting.

Mme. Bartholdi turned to Philippe and said, "Would you like something else, Philippe? Your soup is getting cold."

"Oh no, madame. I was just thinking about what M. Bartholdi told me in the studio. 'Open your eyes and your ears. Develop your senses.' I have never seen anyone eat soup the way you did, sideways without noise. And these spoons! Now I know where M. Bartholdi got his idea for constructing the statue in four sizes. He looked at his spoons." Philippe looked at her with great seriousness and then lined his spoons up, largest to smallest.

M. Bartholdi started to laugh. Mme. Bartholdi laughed also.

"Did I say something wrong?" asked Philippe innocently.

"Not at all, Philippe," answered Mme. Bartholdi. "It was impolite of us to laugh. But my husband never told me that was where he took the idea of making the Liberty in four sizes. It never occurred to me."

Bartholdi winked at his wife and said, "But, ma petite chou (*my dearest*), I have often mentioned to you that spoons and statues are nearly the same. Any artist would recognize that. It requires some imagination. You see, Philippe *must* be an artist with great imagination!"

From then on the meal seemed less formal. Philippe had won the hearts of the Bartholdis. And the Bartholdis made him feel welcome. It was the first of many meals Philippe took with the sculptor and his wife over the years.

"Perhaps sometime you could join us again," Mme. Bartholdi said to Philippe as she finished her coffee. "We have no children and have enjoyed immensely your fresh way of seeing things. You have been a perfect guest."

After dinner and conversation in the parlor, M. Bartholdi and Philippe went down to the street. The sculptor called a carriage taxi for Philippe. "Take this boy home please, driver," he said as he gave the driver some money. "He lives at..."

"Twenty-one rue Blaise Pascal," said Philippe. Philippe climbed into the carriage and waved to Bartholdi. "Thank you, monsieur," he said. It was the first time Philippe had ridden in a carriage. There he sat, alone, a young man-about-town and only eleven years old. It was a perfect way to end an eye-opening and exciting evening.

Naturally his parents were waiting up for him when he arrived home. Babette was asleep because it was already 9:45 p.m.

"Well, Philippe, tell us about your evening with M. and Mme. Bartholdi. Was dinner delicious?" asked his mother.

"Maman, do you know that rich people eat with four spoons? And we were served by a woman wearing a uniform. And we spoke about art and politics and imagination and many other things that I did not understand," Philippe continued on breathlessly.

"Papa, I saw M. Bartholdi's studio. It was fantastique! Extra-ordinaire!! He has enough ideas for statues to keep all the coppersmiths in Paris busy forever!"

M. Peden puffed on his large porcelain and wood tobacco pipe. He blew out a smoke ring which quivered in the air. "You have rubbed elbows with the best, Philippe. We are very happy that M. Bartholdi and his wife invited you. You must be proud of yourself. We are."

"And Bartholdi himself called a carriage to take me home. Oh, Papa, it is... I am so excited... and they have invited me to have supper with them again," Philippe added.

Philippe's mother hugged him. "That is wonderful, Philippe. Isn't it, Papa?"

His papa looked at him sternly and blew another smoke ring that hung in the air. "Now just don't become a snob, Philippe. Remember, in this house, we eat with one spoon!" M. Peden laughed and so did Philippe.

The work progressed as usual in the workshop through 1881 and into the next year. On October 24, 1881, the American ambassador, Levi Morton, was asked to drive the first rivet into the large toe of the statue's left foot. It seemed like an odd and comical way to celebrate, but Bartholdi knew that it was necessary to involve the Americans, who were taking their own good time in finding enough money to build the pedestal. Philippe, his father, and all the workers were there for the ceremony.

At a ceremony planned for the occasion, the first rivet is driven into the left foot of the statue. The assembly process can now begin.

CHAPTER FOUR

ERECTING LIBERTY

Back to back, Philippe and his father were almost the same height. Philippe was tall for a boy of thirteen. Perhaps being a hardworking apprentice for three years had stretched him out. He was even nearly as tall as Jean.

"You know, it's hard to imagine how this statue will look when she is clothed in her copper skin," said Jean.

"Oh, I can picture it, Jean," said Philippe. "But I think what *will* be a surprise to everyone will be how big she will look."

"I wonder what that fellow is doing over there," Jean said, pointing to a short, bearded man with a strange-looking three-legged device in front of him.

"That is M. Gontrand. He is the photographer M. Bartholdi told me about. He will take photographs of the erection of the statue in the courtyard," Philippe explained. "That way there will be a record of how it was done. One day, people will look at his photographs and they will say, 'Oh, that is the way they did it!'"

"Shall we go down and see what he is doing?" asked Jean.

"Let's finish our lunch first," said Philippe.

Philippe and Jean always chose to have their lunch in the strangest places. Today, they were eating their bread and cheese while standing in the head of the statue. The head, which had been set in the courtyard after the 1878 Exposition, was a good, quiet place, away from the din of hammers and saws. The boys would lean out the windows of the crown and throw small balls of bread down to the watchman's cat. From their high perch they could see everything — visitors arriving, huge, gray workhorses pulling wagons loaded with iron bars. It was a great, private spot to see without being seen.

They walked down the spiral staircase of the head into the courtyard. Philippe and Jean greeted the photographer who was ready to take a picture.

"Bonjour, monsieur (*hello, sir*)," said Philippe.

"Oh hello, boys," said the photographer.

"You must be Monsieur Gontrand. Are you going to take a picture of the iron skeleton?" asked Philippe.

"Yes, I am. Now, if you will stand behind me, then I will do my work," Gontrand said gruffly.

He placed a black cloth over his head and covered the wooden camera with the cloth. He snapped the shutter and counted, "Un, deux, trois, quatre, cinq, six, sept, huit…" Then he removed the film plate and took another film plate and repeated the process.

"Do you think, Monsieur Gontrand, that we can look through the camera?" asked Jean shyly.

"I suppose so," said Gontrand. "Only don't touch anything. Anything! Did you hear what I said?"

Jean was first. "Hey, it's upside down, Philippe. Something is wrong with the camera."

"Let me see," said Philippe, pushing Jean aside. Philippe

looked. "You're right, Jean. It *is* upside down. How can that be?" asked Philippe.

"It only looks that way in the camera. It is quite all right, I assure you," said Gontrand.

And this is what Philippe and Jean saw through the camera:

"Good-bye boys," the photographer said. "I will see you in a few months when there is more of the statue to be seen."

"Au revoir, Monsieur Gontrand," replied Jean and Philippe.

"Strange fellow," said Jean.

"He has to be strange. In his profession, everything is upside down," said Philippe.

The torch and the arm had been on exhibit in New York and Philadelphia for nearly seven and a half years. Toward the end of the spring of 1883, it was returned to Paris. It had spent much of its time in fashionable Madison Square Park in New York City. The American Pedestal Committee thought exhibiting the torch would be a good way to remind people to donate money to fund the construction of the stone pedestal on which the statue was to stand in New York harbor.

It was difficult to imagine a statue which would rise above the rooftops of Paris!

Work continued briskly in Paris. Eiffel finished the iron armature for the arm. He put it in place. The pieces of the torch were taken out of twenty-one crates and reassembled. The torch looked a little worn, since it was the oldest part of Liberty. The railing was shiny from so many hands gripping it.

One morning, Bartholdi called together the coppersmiths and metalworkers and all the other craftsmen in the court-yard in front of the iron skeleton. He stood next to the base of the statue and spoke in a booming voice: "Craftsmen of Liberty, we have reached a turning point in our work. We have finished hammering the last copper sheet! For many of you, the work is done. You have made history here at 25 rue de Chazelles. *We* have made history together. Never before has such a statue been built by people: the common citizens of France, who have contributed money, and the men who have poured their sweat into her wood and copper. We have not only made ourselves proud, but we have, more impor-tantly, made France proud!!"

People in the crowd shouted "Vive Bartholdi!" "Vive Eiffel!" "Vive la Liberté!!!"

Bartholdi cleared his throat and continued. "Tomorrow we begin mounting the copper sheets on the framework. Vive la France!!" Bartholdi embraced Eiffel and all the workers threw their hats into the air.

It seemed like a miracle. The huge copper sections that had been made, one by one, fit together beautifully. From the feet up, she rose majestically, with every intricate gleaming fold of her monumental robe glowing in the sunlight. The workmen scurried on the wooden scaffolding. More pieces were raised and riveted together.

"Monsieur Bartholdi, why do we leave a small overlap between the pieces?" Philippe asked one day.

"Well, Philippe that is a good question, and there is a good reason. As you know, copper, like any metal, expands or contracts, depending on the temperature. When the sun is beating down, the copper pieces will expand and on cold days the copper will contract. That is why there must be a small space for this invisible movement."

"I didn't realize that when we were hammering the sheets. But now that you mention it, it's true," said Philippe.

"Perhaps what is even more strange is that theoretically, the statue could become a huge electric battery. You see, Philippe, the iron braces and skeleton will react chemically with the copper sheets. If you remember, before we attached the iron to the copper, we put cloth coated in asbestos between the iron and copper. The cloth will act as an insulator. This way, if it is struck by lightning in a thunderstorm, the statue will not be electrically charged."

This is how Eiffel's superstructure and architect Richard Hunt's granite pedestal would look together.

"I have been working on this statue for three years and there are still things about it I do not know," said Philippe.

"Let me show you something else, Philippe," said Bartholdi, unrolling a large architectural drawing on a table. "This is the plan for the granite pedestal that will hold our statue. It has been designed by the great American architect Richard Hunt. I believe it is precisely what is needed."

"How high will the pedestal be?" asked Philippe.

"Hunt suggests that it should rise 114 feet, but it will probably be shortened to about 90 feet. Altogether, the statue and pedestal will be over 300 feet tall. It will be taller than any other structure in America!" exclaimed Bartholdi.

"Do you think the pedestal will be ready when our work is done?" asked Philippe.

"That is the big question now," said Bartholdi quietly. "I am afraid not. Only last week, they broke ground for the base inside the old fort on the island. The statue may have to wait in Paris for quite a while until the Americans raise the money for the pedestal. In the meantime we shall enjoy the statue while we have it. I am planning a little party for her in July."

"A party?" asked Philippe.

"Yes. I shall invite journalists, prominent citizens, members of foreign embassies, my wife, and my mother. You will also be there — our star apprentice!" said Bartholdi.

M. Gontrand returned during the first week of July. He set up his camera and waited for the sun, which was playing hide and seek with the clouds. On his lunch break, Philippe spotted the photographer.

"Monsieur Gontrand, how are you? Ready to take another photograph?" asked Philippe.

"How can I," he said, pulling at his hair. "Look at this... this mess. Copper sheets lying helter-skelter, piles of boards... The picture will look ugly."

"But this is a workshop, not a museum, monsieur," said Philippe.

"Don't be impertinent with me, boy. Go and fetch M. Bartholdi. I demand to speak with him," said Gontrand, almost screaming.

Philippe found M. Bartholdi in the workshop. "Excuse me, sir, but M. Gontrand, the photographer, is here and is ready to take a photograph in the courtyard. He is upset about something and he wants to speak with you personally," explained Philippe.

"Very well, Philippe. He is always upset about something. He thinks when he photographs something he actually creates the thing he photographs! Come, let's speak with Mr. High and Mighty!" said Bartholdi, laughing.

M. Gontrand was standing there with folded arms and a sour face. He shouted, "Alors, Monsieur Bartholdi! Que se passe t-il? (*Oh, M. Bartholdi! What is happening here?*)"

"Calm down, my friend. There is no need to be so angry. I know you want to create the best photograph possible, but I have a statue to put up. We shall clear up some of this debris. All right?" Bartholdi patted Gontrand on the back reassuringly and shook his hand.

Within ten minutes "the mess" was cleared away.

"Is it all right for the two men to be in the torch?" asked Philippe.

"Yes, yes, they don't bother me," said Gontrand, and then he shouted across the courtyard to the men in the torch, "Ne bougez pas! (*Don't move!*)" And the men waved and answered, "D'accord (*O.K.*)."

"Un, deux, trois, quatre, cinq, six, sept..." and click! "Excellent," said M. Gontrand.

The photograph that was developed showed the copper sheathing half way up. Two workers stand in the torch.

A week later the plans for the party were set. The carpenters built a temporary floor at the level of Liberty's knee. Once the floor was complete, chairs and tables were hoisted up by rope and pulley. Philippe watched these unusual events. He had a big smile on his face. The idea seemed crazy. Lunch inside a statue's knee! But, who knows? It might just work.

"Well, what do you think of my foolishness, Philippe?" asked Bartholdi, walking over to the apprentice.

"Oh, monsieur. You startled me. It is very… very… imaginative," said Philippe, finding the right word.

"I am glad you like it, my young friend," Bartholdi said as he watched the last of the chairs rise up into the knee of the statue. "There is something I have been meaning to give to you, Philippe."

Bartholdi dug his hand into his pocket and came up with something shiny. "Voilà! (*Here it is!*)," said the sculptor, opening his hand. He held three rectangular pieces of copper on which were engraved "Fragment de cuivre de la Statue Colossal de la Liberté executée par A. Bartholdi, 1875–1883 — Souvenir d'une visite aux travaux. *(A piece of copper from the colossal Statue of Liberty built by A. Bartholdi, 1875–1883 — Souvenir of a visit to the foundry.)*"

*T*he copper souvenir which Bartholdi gave to Philippe.

"These are for you. I have signed them myself," said Bartholdi, pointing to his signature on the left.

"But why all three? I am only one person!" said Philippe.

"Do you not have a sister named Babette?" said Bartholdi.

"Why, yes," said Philippe.

"She would be jealous if she did not receive one. N'est-ce-pas? (*Isn't that right?*)," said the sculptor.

"And the third one?" asked Philippe.

"Someday you will have a child or a grandchild who will want to know about the statue. That piece is for him or her." Bartholdi looked at Philippe and shook his hand.

Champagne and food had been arriving all morning. Waiters began unpacking the food and drink, which the workmen hauled up to the table in Liberty's knee. Thirty guests were expected. Bartholdi climbed the long ladder to inspect the table and other preparations. "What a spectacular view for a luncheon!" he said, admiring the rooftops of the neighboring buildings.

As the guests arrived, they were brought to the base of the statue, where they were all served a glass of champagne. "Ladies and gentlemen," said Bartholdi, standing on Liberty's left foot. "I wish to propose a toast. To my mother, who inspired the face of Liberty and to my wife, who inspired the rest." Everyone laughed and toasted as they raised their glasses: "To Liberty, long may she stand!"

"Now if you will follow me, please. And please do not look down," said Bartholdi on the ladder. One by one they climbed the wooden ladder which rose at least 40 feet from the ground. A special rope chair had to be used to hoist Bartholdi's aged mother, but Jeanne-Emilie refused to use the rope chair. She went up the ladder, like all the male guests. Philippe was one of the last, after the journalists and politicians. He had been chosen by Bartholdi to represent the workers.

When he reached the knee, Philippe could not believe what he saw: the most elegantly laid table, with silverware, porcelain plates, and crystal glasses. A huge oval table with thirty chairs filled the center of the "room." There was even enough space for the waiters to walk around and serve. After all the guests were seated, Bartholdi gave a signal to the six waiters, who each opened a champagne bottle at the same time. The corks (each with small blue, white, and red streamers attached) flew straight up through the iron skeleton, or out the sides. Bartholdi rose, clinked his glass with his fork handle, and spoke, "May I thank you all for rising to the occasion of Liberty! (*Laughter*). I wish to present to the press and to our assembled, distinguished guests Mme. Charlotte Beysser Bartholdi, whose face Liberty shall wear forever." Bartholdi held his mother's hand as she stood up to his right. She was a woman dressed completely in black, and her stern but beautiful face had the same distant stare as that of the statue. No smile crossed her lips, nor did she say a word. She gracefully sat down.

Next Bartholdi introduced his wife: "A sculptor could not wish for a more beautiful model, nor a more beautiful wife. It is even better when they are one and the same person. May I present Mme. Jeanne-Emilie Bartholdi, upon whose enlarged knee you dine today." All the guests roared with laughter as Jeanne-Emilie curtsied and sat down.

The meal was brought up to the platform by a rope-and-pulley system, with roasted chickens being hoisted four stories before they were served. "This is probably the highest a chicken has ever flown," said one journalist to a consul. Laughter and the clinking of glasses were heard far below in the courtyard. The workers had been given the day off, and so there was no other sound but the noise of the guests having a joyous time.

Course after course followed. Bartholdi stood up again, a little tipsy from the champagne. "No doubt you have questions about the statue. Fire away, gentlemen. Now is your

"May I thank you all for rising to the occasion of Liberty!"

chance before we finish this colossal restaurant (*laughter*)... I mean, statue."

"How large is the face, Monsieur Bartholdi?" asked a reporter from *Harper's Weekly*.

"Ten feet across, sir. The nose is 4½ feet long. Each eye is 2½ feet long."

"When will she be finished?" asked another American from *Frank Leslie's Illustrated Newspaper*.

Bartholdi thought for a moment and said, "You may write this in your newspapers. By next July 4, your Independence Day, I promise that we will be able to present a completed statue to your country. But the question is, 'Will America be ready to receive her?'"

"Monsieur Bartholdi, it has been rumored that you have neither asked for nor accepted any financial compensation for your work on this statue. Is this true, sir?" asked the gentleman from *The London Illustrated*.

"When you are in love, the object of your love is payment enough. Sir, for me creating the statue is a labor of love. I look at it and see my dear wife and my beloved mother. What else could any man want but to have such a combination — 151 feet tall!!" said Bartholdi cleverly.

The guests cheered and applauded. Their laughter echoed through the hollow cave-like body of the statue. More champagne corks were shot through the iron skeleton into the air.

The surprise of the party was about to be revealed. With a short drumroll and a blast from a trumpet, four waiters carried out a 4-foot high Statue of Liberty cake of confectioner's sugar. It looked like the real thing — a white statue of sugar! Everyone gasped. The guests cheered in delight. It was truly the crowning moment of a wonderful celebration.

But Bartholdi realized that the days that lay ahead of this brief and pleasant afternoon would be no party. The problems he would soon encounter would test his patience.

A PEDESTAL FOR LIBERTY

Just as Bartholdi and his coppersmiths in Paris were attaching Liberty's copper skin to her iron framework, orders in New York were issued to begin work at Bedloe's Island. The American Pedestal Committee finally had enough money in its bank account to begin the long and difficult task of preparing the place where Liberty was to stand.

Old Fort Wood on Bedloe's Island had been chosen by Bartholdi himself when he had visited America in 1871. You might say he had fallen in love with the little island. From his ship's deck, he could see the overgrown ruins of an abandoned fort on the small island. He knew instinctively that a colossal statue would fit perfectly inside the fort. It had all the right elements: it was open to the sky from all points of the compass; it was surrounded by water; yet it was close enough to be seen from land and passing ships. What more could he want? To the sculptor, Bedloe's Island was made for the statue. And the statue he built was designed for that place alone. But twelve years were to pass before government approvals were given and the work on the pedestal was to begin.

And what work!! The stone walls of the fort, which had been built around 1800, were in a terrible state of disrepair. Years of neglect and weather had loosened the mortar. Even the docks on the island needed to be rebuilt so that large ships and barges could use them on a daily basis. The fort, in the shape of an eleven-pointed star, surely needed work if the colossal statue were to stand proudly in its center. General Charles Stone, the engineer-in-chief of the pedestal project, and Richard Hunt, the architect of the pedestal, visited the island and walked over the parade ground of the fort.

"How deep will you excavate, General Stone?" asked Mr. Hunt.

"That depends on what we find. This fort was used for many things. There is no telling what we will encounter. But I calculate that we will have to go down at least 20 feet," answered General Stone.

"Well, sir, I shall be here when you need me. Poured concrete for the foundation, you say. It will have to be the most solid piece of concrete ever erected," said Hunt.

"Mr. Hunt, I will construct this foundation and base so soundly, that if the pedestal and statue should ever fall, which it won't, the entire island will turn upside down with it!" said Stone.

The two men laughed. "That would make us both look foolish," said Hunt, laughing.

Within two weeks, wooden barracks were built on the island. These were to house the workers, many of whom were immigrants who had just arrived from Ireland and Italy. Horses and wagons were brought out by barge to help with the heavy, dirty work of removing debris from inside the fort. And so, the work began.

No sooner had the workers dug down a few feet, when they hit metal and concrete. During the following weeks and months, the workers pulled out old water tanks, and they dug up bombproof powder magazines, where explosives and ammunition had been stored. Down they continued more than 20 feet, until they hit bedrock. It took five months, considerably longer than had been orginally estimated and much more costly.

By September, the stonemasons and concrete workers arrived. It was time for them to begin filling up the huge hole, which now measured 91 square feet and more than 2 stories deep. These workers, like those who had cleared the rubble from the fort, were also recent immigrants, mainly from Italy. Many had been in the United States for only two or three months. Some, like eleven-year-old Vincent Tomaso and his father, Anthony, from Turin, Italy, had been in the States for a year.

"Vincent, you hold my hand, now, and don't get lost," said Anthony, a short, stocky man with a thick moustache, black hair, and a heavy accent.

"Don't worry, Papa. I'll be O.K. Is this where we are going to live and work? Mama would love this little island."

"She'll see it when she comes over with your two sisters — maybe in a year, when we can send her tickets," said Mr. Tomaso.

"Come, Papa, let's see where we are going to stay," said Vincent, tugging at his father's sleeve.

Vincent and his father followed the other workers, suitcases and bags in hand, to the wooden houses on the other side of the island. They entered a long, unpainted wooden building with ten beds along the two walls.

"What a big family," Vincent said, looking at his father.

"You take this bed, Vincent. I'll sleep in the bed next to yours," said Anthony. The room was filled with men of all sizes. Vincent was the only boy and the only apprentice. It was a different way of life but they would get used to it. The whole place began to seem like, well, not like home... but it was too early to say.

*S*ome, like eleven-year-old Vincent Tomaso and his father, Anthony, from Turin, Italy, had been in the States for a year.

The thing Vincent enjoyed most was walking down to the shore and skipping flat stones over the water's surface. Across the harbor rose New York City, the largest city in America. Every few minutes, three masted ships and paddlewheelers passed the island. Nothing was boring, especially the work.

A large steam engine stood near the top of the pit. It was fired with coal that had been left beneath the fort in huge quantities during the Civil War. Throughout the day the engine chugged and coughed as it mixed sackfuls of cement with buckets of sand and gravel from nearby New Jersey and Staten Island. Horses pulled wagons over a small railway, which had been built to connect the docks to the pit. Another steam engine pumped saltwater from the harbor. With occasional puffs of black smoke, the engines worked all day long, chugging, mixing, and pumping the sand, gravel, water, and cement that were needed to make concrete.

Layer after layer, the concrete was poured into the pit, which had been lined with heavy, roughly cut wooden timbers to give the concrete a form. Throughout the fall and into the cold winter, day after day, week after week, the work continued until the pit was filled and work started on the base. In the middle of the base, iron beams were placed in the concrete to help anchor the pedestal and the statue.

They put in ten hours of work every day except Sunday — long, hard, backbreaking work! General Stone was pleased with the progress, even though they were still behind schedule. The walls of the base rose — 20 feet of thick concrete that was as solid as the Rock of Gibraltar! Then things came to a grinding halt! The American Pedestal Committee had run out of money. It was the first of many such unfortunate instances in which there were not enough funds to continue the work.

Bartholdi had been expecting this bad news for some time. He was pleased that the work on the island had actually begun, but the schedule was a mess. His own timetable was in good shape, however. The statue was now almost finished. M. Gontrand, the photographer, returned with his wooden camera to take another photograph, only this time he was more pleasant.

When it was almost complete in Paris, the statue was hard to see behind its scaffolding.

Meanwhile, Vincent and his father sat in the mess hall on Bedloe's Island eating their breakfast. Of the original fifty workers, less than half remained. No money, no workers — it was as simple as that.

"But, Papa, there is still so much to do. Why have so many of the workers left?" asked Vincent.

"They have families, and they need money to support them. Soon General Stone will find the money. This is a big, rich country. They can't leave this concrete base half finished," explained Anthony. And he was right!

Donations trickled in and the concrete base started to rise again — 30 feet, 35 feet, 40 feet! Additional iron girders stuck out from the top of the base. They were connected to the iron beams in the concrete foundation. By the end of March, 1884, the concrete base rose 45 feet above the ground. More than twenty-five thousand tons of concrete had been used, making this the single largest piece of concrete poured up to that time.

Workmen stand in front of the pedestal's foundation on Bedloe's Island.

61

There was no real celebration, just time for a photograph to be taken and a little speech from General Stone to the assembled workers: "Men, the first part of our work is done, and well done, I might add. It has been far more difficult than we expected. But there wasn't a single injury! You have accomplished a first — never before has so much concrete been put into one place. Some of you will move on to other jobs. I hope that as soon as we are ready to continue with the granite, you will return here. I guarantee that every one of you will be offered work!" As General Stone raised his hand at the end of the rousing speech, the workers cheered.

After the speech, General Stone called Anthony and Vincent over to speak to him. "Tomaso, you and your son are among the best and most trusted workers. I want to make you a foreman. I understand that you are a master stonemason and that you are very familiar with granite work. I will need you when we begin. I will need you as a foreman. You speak the language of the workers better than I." Stone shook Anthony's hand and Anthony smiled. Stone continued, "In fact, I would like both of you to take a trip with me to the quarry at Leete's Island in Connecticut. We should discuss the methods we will use to finish the pedestal."

"My son and I are ready to go with you, General. I like working in granite. It is one of the most beautiful stones with which to build a monument," said Anthony Tomaso.

General Stone, Anthony, Vincent, and the architect Richard Hunt boarded a small schooner and sailed to the quarry. The trip was calm and pleasant. During the entire trip, the boat stayed within sight of the Connecticut shoreline as it sailed up the Long Island Sound. Little white-washed villages dotted the shore. Finally they reached the quarry, which was set into the rocky beach.

"Of all the samples we have seen, the granite from this quarry is by far the most dense and uniform in its gray color. It is also close to New York, so that all the stone can be loaded into a scow to be sent down to the island," said Hunt.

"Do they have good workers here, General, who know how to work the stone?" asked Anthony.

"Excellent, Mr. Tomaso. Many are your countrymen. They are able to achieve a fine mirror finish on the granite that is second to none."

"Papa, what is that?" asked Vincent, pointing to a huge crane.

General Stone answered, "Vincent, that is a steam-driven derrick that lifts the huge, heavy, uncut blocks onto large wagons. These blocks can weigh eight tons or more. A team of four oxen pulls each wagon over to the water's edge to those small huts and tents, where the granite is shaped and cut to size. Then it is dressed and pointed and chiseled with sharp metal chisels, if it is a rough surface you want."

"Some of the blocks we will use will have a rough surface, Vincent," said Mr. Hunt. "Others must be smooth as glass."

"And when the granite blocks are ready, they are put on a huge sanding machine, where they are sanded to remove the nicks and rough spots. Then they are polished with different kinds of grits. It is dangerous work because the tiny chips of stone can easily fly into your eyes," said General Stone.

"You know a lot about this place, don't you," said Vincent to General Stone. "I guess that's how you got your name — General Stone."

Mr. Hunt and General Stone roared with laughter. Vincent's father laughed uncomfortably. Vincent smiled sheepishly.

"You have a clever boy, Mr. Tomaso," said General Stone.

They walked over to the chipping tent, where stonecutters were working on a rough-faced block of granite. Mr. Tomaso spoke Italian to one of the workers. Then he explained to Mr. Hunt and the General what the worker had told him. "He says that this is a much tougher and denser granite than we have in Italy. It is harder to work with and takes more time.

The steam driven derrick lifts the heavy blocks of stone onto the wagon pulled by oxen.

The granite was brought to the chipping tent where it was smoothed and polished.

This fellow comes from a village not far from mine in the north near Turin."

At the docks, immense pieces of polished granite were being loaded onto flat-bottomed scows. On board, a steam engine connected to a crane lifted each block onto the deck.

"When do you want to start, Mr. Hunt?" asked Anthony.

"It's up to our engineer, General Stone," Hunt said.

"I'm afraid it is up to the committee. They are low on funds again," said Stone.

"I have a feeling," said Hunt, "that the pedestal I designed at 114 feet will be too expensive. I may have to shorten it by about 25 feet," said Hunt.

"It might be the only way to get things started again," said Stone, thinking about the future.

Meanwhile in Paris, Philippe and his father were putting Liberty's head on her shoulders, and her arm and torch on the iron skeleton.

"I think that the promise M. Bartholdi made last year about the statue being ready by July 4 will be kept," said Philippe to his father as they sat on top of the crown.

"Philippe, you are probably right. I wonder what will happen to the statue after it is given to the Americans on the Fourth of July?"

"M. Bartholdi says it will stay here until the pedestal is ready. He does not want to embarrass them!" said Philippe.

Down on the ground at the foot of the statue, Bartholdi was speaking to his assistant, M. Simon. "Let's contact the French Statue Committee and the American Embassy. Let's tell them that we shall be ready to officially give them the statue on American Independence Day."

"Do you think that we can make it, M. Bartholdi?" asked M. Simon.

"We must. A promise is a promise. History will show that we were ready when we said we would be. Perhaps the Americans will be forced into action."

As the Fourth of July approached, the workshop bustled with activity. Additional workers were hired to clean up the wood and metal strewn about the workshop and to clear up the debris in the courtyard. A striped refreshment tent was set up. French and American flags and banners were draped on poles and across the sides of the work sheds. Carpenters began removing the scaffolding from around the head and the torch. The timbers were hauled down to build the platform on which the celebration would take place. It would be a grand send-off for the statue.

At 11:00 A.M. on that bright and sunny summer morning, the decorated gates of the Gaget and Gauthier foundry were flung open to the waiting crowds. Hundreds of elegantly dressed guests, joined by scores of workers who had helped to build the statue, filed in. People in neighboring buildings and houses jammed the rooftops. A band in the courtyard tuned up.

Count de Lesseps, the head of the French Statue Committee, spoke first. At the end of his speech, he turned to Mr. Levi Morton, the American ambassador to France and said, "Our French Statue Committee now hereby transfers to you, as the representative of the United States, this Statue of Liberty as a pledge of friendship between our two countries." De Lesseps opened up a gold box from which he removed a rolled-up parchment tied with a blue, white, and red ribbon. He handed the parchment to Morton.   .

Then Morton spoke, "God grant that it may stand until the end of time as an emblem of our two great nations."

A great shout was heard. The deed was done. Champagne flowed. Workers embraced each other. Philippe and his father watched with tears in their eyes, for it was a happy event mixed with a feeling of sadness. Sadness, because the

On July 4, 1884, the Statue of Liberty was officially given to the Americans.

Liberty would soon leave its place of birth in Paris to be shipped to America.

A month later in America, on August 5, the six-ton granite cornerstone held suspended in the air by a crane was ready to be laid. The weather was miserable. A hard rain fell on the few hundred people gathered on Bedloe's Island. Underneath the stone, two workers placed into the concrete foundation a historical time capsule: a copper box filled with

67

It rained heavily the day that the cornerstone was laid into the pedestal.

coins and medals, a copy of the Declaration of Independence, and the history of the statue. The granite block was then lowered. Finally it seemed, the work on the pedestal was to begin.

Vincent, his father, and the other stonemasons started the next day. The stone blocks were unloaded from the scow and placed onto a small railway car pulled by horses. Cranes and derricks were erected to hoist the heavy stones, some of which were three feet thick. Things were going smoothly. But, just as it seemed that everything was going well, the pockets of the American Pedestal Committee were empty once again.

It appeared that the statue would have to remain in Paris after all, at least until the spring of 1885. But Bartholdi didn't seem to mind. Thousands of visitors were drawn to the curious colossal statue standing in the middle of Paris. Artists painted it. Newspaper reporters wrote about it. Everyone grew accustomed to it. By winter it was blanketed with a dusting of light snow.

One cold, snowy Sunday, Bartholdi and Jeanne-Emilie paid a visit to the statue. As they approached the workshop they recognized Philippe standing near the gates.

"Is that you, Monsieur Bartholdi, Madame Bartholdi?" asked Philippe, surprised to see the sculptor.

"We thought we would look at 'our daughter,' Philippe. What are you doing here?" asked Bartholdi.

"I come here every Sunday. I guess I will until it is time to send her to America. She grows more mysterious and more beautiful every day. Sometimes, when the cold wind blows hard, you can hear the metal creak. It is almost as if she is talking," said the apprentice.

"I feel sad that she will leave us," said Jeanne-Emilie, "but it must be. She was destined to be an American."

"But we shall enjoy her last few months in Paris, won't we dear?" said Bartholdi. "Philippe, there is something I would like to ask you. When the statue goes to America, they will need some skilled coppersmiths there to make sure that the statue has not suffered during its long trip. General Stone has asked me to send someone who will be able to advise the Americans in piecing the statue together. M. Eiffel and I cannot go, since we have other projects to do. Do you think you and your father would be willing to go to America and live and work on Bedloe's Island during the erection of the statue?" Bartholdi finished speaking and awaited an answer earnestly.

"I am ready to go now," said Philippe, without thinking. "I shall ask Papa, but I believe he will agree. Thank you Monsieur Bartholdi, Madame. Good day to you both."

In the spring of 1885, an American newspaper publisher by the name of Joseph Pulitzer, himself an immigrant, decided to take things into his own hands. He was tired of hearing excuses that the American Pedestal Committee could not raise the needed funds. He promised in an article in his paper, *The World,* that he would collect $100,000. He promised that he would print the name of everyone who donated money.

As if by magic, money started to pour in: allowances from children, dimes and quarters from new immigrants and store clerks. From all over the country, money was sent to *The World.* Pulitzer kept his word; he printed the names of all the contributors and he started to sell tens of thousands of subscriptions to the paper. Liberty was actually good for business!

Work began again on Bedloe's Island in early May. Pulitzer's campaign was working, reaching every corner of America. Bartholdi received a telegram telling him that work on the pedestal was under way once again. He gave immediate orders for the statue, which had already been placed into crates to be sent to the States. From the Paris workshop it traveled by wagon to the railway station in Paris, where it was sent by train to the port of Rouen. There, the 215 crates were loaded onto the *Isere,* a French naval ship. The ship sailed out into the English Channel and began its transatlantic journey.

After a stormy voyage, the statue was welcomed with full fanfare, sea parades, and ceremonies in New York harbor. The crates were placed onto barges and brought to Bedloe's Island where they were stored in wooden sheds. By the end of August, the full $100,000 had been successfully raised, and the work on the pedestal went into full swing. A double shift worked at the quarry. Vincent and Anthony were back to working ten hours a day. Additional stonemasons were hired.

On Sundays, visitors came from near and far by excursion

*N*ew York City salutes the arrival of the steamship Isère *with its cargo of the world's largest statue.*

boats to see the pedestal under construction. These were the days when Vincent and his father went to church in New York City and, later in the afternoon, usually went for a walk up Fifth Avenue. Afterwards they went to a restaurant on Grand Street for a good Italian meal.

It was 1885, the year in which America became serious about its gift of the Liberty statue. But there was still much more to do.

NEW YORK'S LIBERTY

Despite the snow and the wind that chilled the stonemasons to the bone, the pedestal continued to rise steadily through the winter of 1885. Along the shoreline of Bedloe's Island, ice floes from the Hudson River piled up. Sometimes the scow from the quarry had a treacherous time docking because of ice chunks as large as wagons. The cold air was brutal. From the horses' nostrils, snorts of steam broke the crisp, frigid air. It made the horses look like steam engines!

"I don't know which is harder, working in summer or in winter," said Vincent, stamping his feet and trying to keep warm.

"The cold is always worse," said Anthony. "You are always aching. The mortar freezes, and the cement doesn't mix well. The days are shorter with less light, so you have to work in the dark in the morning. Give me the summer anytime."

"How is it going, Tomaso?" asked General Stone, arriving at the pedestal site.

"Slow, General, very slow. The men complain more than they work. We make little mistakes because of this cold weather. But we are still making progress, sir," said Anthony.

"You're a good foreman, Tomaso. I like your spirit and determination. You will go far in America. How are you, Vincent?" asked General Stone.

"I would be better if the sun was shining," Vincent shivered.

"It will, my boy, it will," said Stone as he hunched down in his heavy military overcoat.

As the winter passed, the tempo of the work quickened. By April, only the last rows of granite remained. The workers pushed harder and worked with renewed energy. On April 22, 1886, a milestone was reached: the very last two-ton granite block hung over its intended place. General Stone who liked to make the most of any ceremony called the men together. Some members of the Pedestal Committee attended. "Gentlemen," he said, "we are one stone away from our mission. We have not lost a single man, nor have we had any injuries among the workers. I would like to lay this last block in silver." People dug into their pockets and threw nickels, dimes, quarters, and silver dollars into the wet mortar. The granite stone was lowered into place.

General Stone congratulated Mr. Hunt. The committee members shook the hands of the workers. Richard Butler, secretary of the Pedestal Committee, patted Vincent on the back.

"Well, lad, how does it feel to have completed this part of the work for Liberty?" asked Butler.

"I am proud that I have helped, Mr. Butler. Now my mother and sisters will be able to come to America. I have worked for their freedom too," said Vincent.

"Well said. I like that. Mr. Tomaso, on behalf of the committee, I wish to thank you for your work as foreman. I understand from General Stone that you will be continuing to work on the island for the summer, supervising the additional masonry work on the walks and the walls of the fort," said Butler.

"That is news to me, sir. But if you are making me an offer, my son and I will not refuse good, honest work. We enjoy it here, working on this island project!" said Anthony.

*   *   *   *   *

"Now take care of your papa, Philippe." Mme Peden looked at her son and her husband and started to cry.

"We'll be fine, Maman. Really, we'll be just fine, won't we, Monsieur Bartholdi?" said Philippe.

"Madame Peden," said Bartholdi, "your husband and your son are going to honor you, themselves, and even all of France. How can the statue be finished in America without a single French worker there? It is impossible. I know I can trust them to put up the statue so that it won't be lopsided or crooked. They know best, believe me," said Bartholdi, standing in the courtyard of the foundry.

A horse and carriage pulled up to the workshop gates. The driver climbed down, said a few words, and placed the suitcases on the back of the carriage on the luggage rack. Philippe kissed his mother and little sister. He embraced Bartholdi. Philippe's father did the same. Philippe and his father climbed into the carriage. Bartholdi came up and spoke through the window.

"After you have examined the pedestal and M. Eiffel's iron framework, send me a telegram. I want to know the progress from someone acquainted with the statue. Mr. Butler of the American Pedestal Committee will take good care of you, Monsieur Peden. Should you need anything, do not hesitate to ask him. Driver, to the train station, if you please." Bartholdi waved at Philippe and M. Peden. He knew that his statue would be in good hands.

Mme. Peden and Babette waved as the horse and carriage clickety-clopped down the cobblestone street. Bartholdi could see that they were crying softly.

"Madame Peden, if you need anything, you can find me in

*M*me. Peden and Babette waved as the horse and carriage clickety-clopped down the cobblestone street.

my studio. I have arranged for you to be able to pick up your husband's wages at the foundry. Good-bye, madame. Good-bye, Babette."

"Thank you for your kindness, Monsieur Bartholdi," said Mme. Peden.

For twelve days, M. Peden and Philippe sailed the Atlantic. It was a new experience for both of them. The crossing was rough, and M. Peden became seasick. He spent many hours lying down in his cabin.

"Papa, you look terrible. Your face is almost green," said Philippe as he sat by his father's side.

"Oh, Philippe! I have been in many places but never one that has caused me to turn green. I guess I look like weathered copper," said M. Peden.

"Well, you do look a little like an old copper roof, Papa. The captain says the weather will be calm in a day or two," added Philippe, trying to cheer up his father.

A day out of New York, the captain's weather prediction proved correct and M. Peden's normal reddish complexion returned to him. He started eating like a man who had not seen food for days, which he hadn't, of course! By the time they sighted land, he was back to his normal robust self. The ship sailed down the coastline of Long Island.

"Papa, look at how green and beautiful the woods and fields and farms look. I thought America was all big cities. It looks a lot like France!" said Philippe.

When their ship finally steamed into New York harbor at the end of the day, they were filled with anticipation.

"Philippe, come quickly. C'est magnifique! (*It's beautiful!*)," said M. Peden, looking towards Bedloe's Island with its fort and pedestal.

"It is the pedestal, just like the pictures M. Bartholdi showed me of M. Hunt's drawings! And the iron skeleton is halfway done. It looks completely different from when we saw it in Paris. Not as big," explained Philippe.

"Bartholdi was right. From a ship, the statue will be seen by everyone arriving in America," said M. Peden.

They were met at the dock by Mr. Butler, who helped them through the customs inspection at Castle Garden, the place where all foreigners were processed.

"Monsieur Peden, I have arranged for you to stay at a hotel for a couple of days. After you have rested and seen the city a little, you can go out to stay on the island. I am sure you are anxious to see how far along the work is. And you must be also, Philippe. M. Bartholdi wrote me about you. I hope you will like America," said Mr. Butler.

As they drove to the hotel, Philippe kept sticking his head out of the carriage window. "It is so big. Everything is immense. And the people rush around like bees. Fantastique!" exclaimed Philippe, whose eyes were nearly popping out of his head.

Two days later, M. Peden, Philippe, and Mr. Butler arrived on Bedloe's Island.

"Where is the statue?" asked Philippe.

"In crates," Mr. Butler answered. "General Stone has been working on the iron framework. We have unpacked a few pieces to see how they managed the voyage. Some spots will need your attention, Monsieur Peden. The wooden crates dented the copper in a few places. You have brought your tools with you, I trust?"

"We have selected about forty different hammers and many other levers and rammers that we thought would be needed. We have come prepared," explained Philippe.

Mr. Butler introduced the Pedens to General Stone, who showed them where they would be staying and set them up in a small shed that he had temporarily made into a copper

The crates containing the statue are transferred on barges because the Isère *was too large to dock at Bedloe's Island.*

workshop. Mr. Butler excused himself, saying that he had to return to his New York office.

After a brief tour of the foundation and pedestal, General Stone introduced the Pedens to the foreman in charge of the ironwork and to Mr. Tomaso and Vincent. At once, Vincent's and Philippe's eyes lit up. Both boys were surprised to find that there was another young person on the island. They soon became fast and close friends, even though communicating with each other required a lot of sign language.

In the coming months, while the iron skeleton was being completed and erected, Philippe, his father, and Vincent began to unpack the many crates. Vincent had received special permission from his father and General Stone to assist the Pedens.

"Philippe, this left foot is going to need some work. There are some bruises near the ankle," said M. Peden.

Philippe and his father went to work in an open-air tent near the shed. By now, Philippe was more than an apprentice. He was sixteen years old, a few years older than Vincent. Now, he was a young man taller than his own father. Philippe had learned coppersmithing well. He knew which hammer to use and how to use it. His father treated him as an equal. It was a pleasure to see them work together. Vincent watched with amazement.

"This is the largest foot I have ever seen," Vincent said. "How many pieces are there to this statue?" he asked.

"About three hundred," said Philippe matter-of-factly.

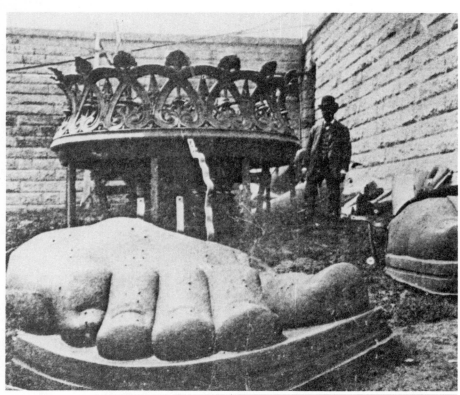

No one had ever seen a foot larger than a person.

"Do you know where they all go?" asked Vincent.

"There is a plan, Vincent. Every piece has numbers written on it to tell where it fits. There won't be any problems!" said Philippe.

Every day at lunchtime, Philippe and Vincent sat on the shoreline and talked. Then they would have a rock skipping contest. At first, Philippe was not nearly as good as Vincent, who had been practicing for two years.

"Nine hops!" Philippe said triumphantly. "That is my best so far."

"I still have twelve," boasted Vincent.

"I will catch up to you, Vincent. Don't worry," said Philippe.

Sometimes after the day's work, the two boys would take an old rowboat out into the harbor and circle the island — just like explorers. Other days they would take a swim, diving off the docks into the bay. The days seemed to pass quickly now that Philippe and Vincent had become very good friends.

The iron skeleton was finished and the copper sheets were ready to be assembled. At first the copper skin went up well. M. Peden and Philippe explained to the other workers how to drive the flat-headed rivets through the copper so that they would not stick out. In a little ceremony, General Stone watched the first rivet enter the foot. It was named after Bartholdi. The second rivet was named after Joseph Pulitzer.

But all the work was not to proceed quite so smoothly. Some of the copper pieces had been mislabeled or incorrectly numbered. The pieces would be hoisted up only to be brought back down to the ground. Sometimes it took ten tries to get the right piece in place. It was frustrating, like putting up a huge jigsaw puzzle in the sky. And it was more difficult, far more difficult than the work in Paris.

On Bedloe's Island the workers did not use a wooden scaffold

Erecting the statue on Bedloe's Island was done without scaffolding. A steam derrick helped lift the pieces into place.

built around the statue. The pedestal made it nearly impossible to erect the wooden scaffold. Instead, steam-driven
cranes were used to lift the huge copper pieces. The workers
sat on bosùns chairs suspended by ropes. (A bosùns chair is
a simple wooden board connected by ropes at either end.)
This was dangerous work, especially when the men had to
work within the great folds of the statue's copper robe. As
the rivets were driven into the statue, the popping sound
they made echoed throughout the hollow copper shell of the
body. Inside, other workers attached the double spiral staircase to the iron framework. Activity inside and outside the
statue continued throughout the summer of 1886.

Philippe and his father continued to unpack the crates,
making repairs on the copper when necessary. Curious
visitors made excursions to the island and had their photographs taken while standing next to the face or crown, or
sitting near the large fingers of the colossal statue.

Visitors loved to pose next to the statue's feet and fingers. Note the railway tracks behind these people.

One day at lunch as Philippe and Vincent sat on the stony beach near the coppersmith's tent, they got to talking about more serious things. "How long has it been since you have seen your mother and sisters?" asked Philippe.

"Three years, maybe," said Vincent. "I don't remember my two sisters very well. Sometimes at night, I dream about the whole family being in a large room where we are eating dinner. I'm a man now, and I have little gifts for my mama and for everyone. I put the gifts on their plates. They open them and cry. My Mama says to me, 'Vincent, you're a big man now, not a boy anymore!' Then she hugs me like she hasn't seen me in a long time. My father tells me to sit in his chair at the head of the table. The chair is too big and I can't reach the table."

Philippe picked up a long thin blade of grass. He put the end in his mouth, munched its sweetness, and thought deeply. He lay back, putting his palms under his head. Clouds, sun, ships, New York, Bartholdi's statue. He thought of his mother and Babette in Paris. He hadn't thought of them in a while because he had been too occupied with new experiences and work. Finally he spoke: "You know Vincent, we are lucky, you and me. Some people would say we aren't, but we are. M. Bartholdi once told me that everything big starts from something small. I didn't understand exactly what he meant when I was ten and just beginning as an apprentice. But I think that I have learned. I have been working on this statue for nearly six years. Now I see what he meant. If we are lucky, we become the people we choose to be. Everything we do, no matter how small, determines who and what we will be when we get older. That is the meaning of liberty — freedom to choose!"

Philippe sat up and looked at Vincent and continued, "Who would have thought that a little boy from Paris, who had never seen anything more than his own neighborhood, would become a coppersmith and travel across the ocean to build a giant statue?"

Vincent picked up a stone and threw it lazily into the water. "Philippe, one day, when we are much older, we will each come back to this island and think about the days we spent on this beach throwing stones into the water. We will show it to our children and maybe our grandchildren, and we will tell them about our work. You will say, 'I once knew a boy named Vincent,' and I will tell them about you."

Philippe looked at Vincent and, without speaking, felt the meaning of his friend's words. "Hey, I found a terrific flat stone that is sure to be a champion skipper," said Philippe. He stood up and waited for a wave to break. He cocked his arm and threw it sideways. Seven, eight, nine, ten, eleven, twelve big hops, and it continued in little skips... fourteen in all!! Each skip made a ripple that disappeared in the waves.

Vincent picked up a stone and threw it lazily into the water.

When the statue was nearly finished, it looked frightening without the head and right arm.

By mid-September, the statue's shoulders were nearly finished. Vincent's and his father's work was completed. It came time for Philippe and Vincent to go their separate ways. "Philippe," said Vincent, "my mother and sisters are coming to America. Papa sent them tickets with the money we saved. When they come, we are going to move to that town right over there. It is called Bayonne. Papa says you can see the statue from the shore of Bayonne."

"That's funny, Vincent," said Philippe. "You know Bayonne is the name of a town in France. I wonder if they named this Bayonne after the French town."

"We will stay with my cousins in New York City until Mama arrives. I am so happy. Let's go for a swim, one last time."

Vincent and Philippe stood on the dock of Bedloe's Island. It was early evening as the sun began to set behind the statue. "See how she is silhouetted against the sky with its streaks of red and pale yellow." A patch of blue slowly darkened as the sun dipped down behind New Jersey. "She is beautiful," said Vincent, looking at the statue. "I will be so proud to tell Mama that I helped build the pedestal."

In the distance the twinkling lights of New York City grew brighter. The shadowy form of the statue rose in front of them.

"Look, Vincent, the first star. Make a wish," said Philippe. "Make a secret wish."

Philippe often thought of Vincent after the other boy had left. He wasn't really lonely, but he missed skipping stones and talking to his younger friend. The last push of work came. The statue's head was lifted into place. Philippe and his father spent hours in the crown riveting the sections of the curly hair and the crown. The hand and the torch were the only pieces left to be installed. They were nearly through!

For a week they had been carefully putting the torch together. The copper flame took extra time to rivet because it had been crushed a little in shipping. At last they finished the torch. It was attached to the long ropes of the cranes and was slowly hoisted all the way up. By the end of the day, it was bolted and riveted to the brace of iron. Only the spiral staircase and some last-minute finishing touches still had to be completed.

M. Peden and Philippe had finished their work. They could now pack up their tools and sleep late the next morning, Saturday, October 23.

"Well, Papa, it must be a miracle. We have done the impossible. Look at her, gleaming in the sun, her torch reflecting every ray of sunlight," said Philippe.

"M. Bartholdi has already arrived, Philippe," said M. Peden. "I believe he should be getting in touch with us. Tonight we shall sleep in New York City. The workers' houses and the workshop will be taken down today for the celebration. See, the platform for the speakers is already going up. Come, let's pack our things and see New York."

DEDICATING LIBERTY

The last one of the 600 thousand rivets used to fasten together the statue was driven in place on the afternoon of Saturday, October 23, 1886. It was an important rivet because it closed the back of the foot and sandal, which had been used by the workers as a convenient door during the erection of the statue. At long last the work on the statue was complete. And just in time, too! For all the arrangements for the great unveiling and dedication of the statue had been set for October 28.

There was a craziness in the air all over New York City. You could feel it everywhere you went. In all his life, Philippe had never seen such happenings. During the short time he and his father had lived in New York while they worked on Bedloe's Island, Philippe had gotten used to the big American city. All through the summer of 1886, "Liberty fever" continued to build. People talked about "the statue" wherever they met. Every day, journalists and newspaper artists visited the island to see the statue under construction. Articles began to appear in the daily as well as the weekly newspapers, reporting on the progress of the statue.

It was natural that people were so excited, for the statue was the largest man-made object in all of America. Shops hung colored pictures of the statue in their windows. She was

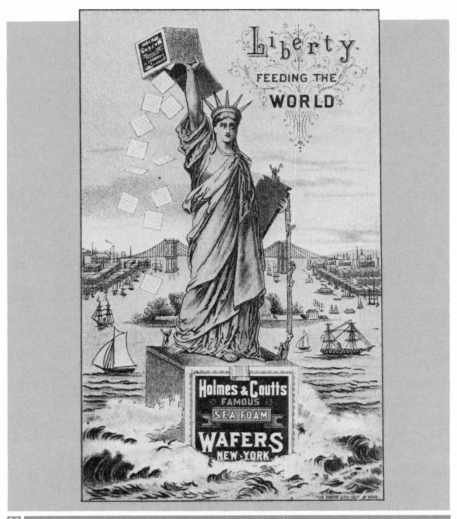

The Statue of Liberty was used in many advertisements like this one, even before it was completed. Such a large statue caught everyone's attention.

even used in advertisements selling sewing machines, thread, medicine, and crackers. Everywhere Philippe looked, the image of the statue was displayed. There was even a hotel named after Bartholdi.

As soon as M. Bartholdi and the entire French delegation arrived in New York the plans for the official dedication went into the full swing. One morning Philippe and his father received a brief note, handwritten by Auguste Bartholdi himself. It read, "You would honor me by coming to the hotel to visit this afternoon at 4:00 p.m. Signed, Bartholdi."

As Philippe and his father sat in the hotel lobby, they looked at the richly dressed hotel guests. They felt a little out of place, even though they wore the best clothes they owned. Bartholdi suddenly appeared, walking quickly toward them. They had never seen him so smartly dressed; he used to come to the workshop in an ordinary floppy bow tie, jacket, and trousers.

"Ah, Monsieur Peden," Bartholdi said, greeting Philippe and his father. M. Peden shook hands with Bartholdi, who embraced him and kissed both cheeks, the way most Frenchmen greet each other. Then Bartholdi kissed Philippe on both cheeks. The sculptor spoke, "You have both done a splendid job erecting the statue. I knew when I sent you to New York earlier this year you would honor the whole workshop and all of France. The statue is fantastique! Greater than my wildest dreams. And bigger too, n'est-ce-pas? (*isn't that right?*) I want you and Philippe to be present on the island for the dedication. Monsieur Peden, you will sit with the other members of our French delegation. Please speak with M. Poirier. He will arrange some suitable clothes for you for the occasion. As for you, my young friend, let's see…" Bartholdi looked at Philippe carefully and smiled, "You have grown as big as the statue since I last saw you. They want *me* to stand in the torch and pull the rope to lift the red, white, and blue banner which will cover Liberty's face. I believe I will be too excited to do the job alone. Could you join me? You will be high in the torch with me."

Philippe could not believe his ears. Six years before, he had been a small child of ten, who carried his father's lunch basket to the workshop and…now he was being asked by the sculptor himself to help unveil the greatest statue in the world.

"I…I…Monsieur Bartholdi…I don't deserve this honor, sir.

I cannot find the words. What can I say?" Philippe said, deeply moved.

"You can say 'yes,'" said Bartholdi clearly and simply.

"Yes, sir, Monsieur Bartholdi," Philippe said loudly, with his heart beating quickly.

"Good! You will not only honor me, but you will honor all the young people of France who contributed their coins and their enthusiasm to our statue." Bartholdi hugged Philippe. Philippe hugged Bartholdi. Bartholdi hugged M. Peden, who hugged him back. Then Philippe and his father hugged each other.

Two elegantly dressed American tourists from Virginia, who happened to be standing nearby, observed this scene. The husband spoke, "They must be French, Emily. Only the French embrace so violently in public!"

Tuesday morning, Philippe and his father were taken by M. Poirier to a ready-to-wear men's clothing shop. They were fitted with the latest in fashion: black formal suit, cravate (tie), white shirt, suspenders, and shoes with buttons.

"Monsieur Poirier," complained Philippe's father, "I have given everything to Liberty, but this…this is too much. I never thought that I, Peden the coppersmith, would ever wear these…these…"

"Clothes," added Poirier. "I have been instructed to outfit you in the fashion of the day. Surely you can do this small thing for Liberty."

"Papa, you look très elegant (*very elegant*)," said Philippe, who was similarly dressed.

"I look like someone else," complained M. Peden. "…And my poor feet will never last in these…these…"

"Shoes," said Poirier. "You will survive, sir. Philippe, you look fine. Now, if you are quite ready, you may change back to your comfortable clothing and we shall leave."

On Wednesday, October 27, the streets were filled with people. Office workers had been given time off to decorate the office buildings along the parade route. Red, white, and blue banners and streamers were hung from the windows. Lampposts were wrapped in colorful ribbons and crepe. The final touches were being put on the reviewing stand. Opposite the World Newspaper building, a huge 60-foot arch decorated with evergreen branches made it look like Christmas. By early evening, New York City looked like a bride before her wedding. Bedloe's Island was also bedecked in colors and all the boats in the harbor were decorated with streamers. For the last few days, the weather had been cool, foggy, and wet. Would it rain on the great day?

That evening as the weather became cooler and mistier, banquets and parties were being held all over the city by the many different military, fire, and police batallions that had come from as far away as Boston and Philadelphia to join in the festivities. Even though it was only a statue in New York's harbor, Americans all over the country had finally taken to the idea of the gift of Liberty from France. It had taken ten long years to accept the idea of the statue and now, on the eve of her dedication, no one was going to miss the grandest show America had ever seen.

Mayor William Grace of New York City proclaimed October 28 "Bartholdi Day." Children were given the day off from school and workers were also given a holiday. Most restaurants and bars remained open and expected business to be brisk.

For a brief period the weather cleared, but only to give people the false hope that the day might be sunny after all. Crowds assembled along the parade route of Fifth Avenue and Broadway, stretching from Fifty-seventh Street, all the way down to the tip of New York opposite the statue.

Philippe and his father, dressed in their fancy clothes, stepped out into a miserable drizzle. "We'd better buy an umbrella," M. Peden suggested as he walked up the street.

His shoes pinched him at every step. Squeaky new shoes and rainy weather — what a combination! But the rest of the crowd was excited, despite the fact that wherever one looked, it was umbrellas and not faces that one saw.

Onlookers hung from lampposts and stuck their heads out the windows of the buildings lining Fifth Avenue. Children were carried on the shoulders of their fathers. New immigrants rubbed elbows with old-time New Yorkers.

"I wonder if Vincent is here?" thought Philippe. "He certainly would not miss this for anything." But the crowds were so dense that it was impossible to recognize anyone. (The newspapers estimated that nearly one million people took part in or observed the day's events. All this in a city with a population of two million.)

In the distance, far up the avenue, the sound of music could be heard. People pushed, trying to catch a better view. And the rain, taking its cue from the music, began to fall. Not a hard, driving rain but a quiet, soaking rain that lasted all day long.

For nearly four hours the parade swept down Fifth Avenue onto Broadway, past City Hall, where President Grover Cleveland and Bartholdi sat on the reviewing stand. Bands from Buffalo and Boston played piece after piece of music. Local marching bands from Brooklyn, Hoboken, and Manhattan were cheered by the onlookers.

Blue-jacketed sailors, red-jacketed firemen, and rows of soldiers, policemen, and politicians arm in arm, all marched in step. Uniformed Civil War veterans and veterans from the War of 1812 and the Mexican War rode past in carriages pulled by chestnut-colored horses. Even a carriage once owned by George Washington was in the parade.

Oh, the noise and trumpets, the firecrackers and yelling, the drums and cheers! New York had never in all its days seen or heard such a tumultuous celebration and all for one statue in the harbor. On they came, one hundred bands in

On October 28, 1886, the Statue of Liberty was dedicated in New York City. Even though it rained all day more than a million people watched the land and sea parades.

all, from Poughkeepsie and Baltimore and other points east and west, north and south. John Philip Sousa, the great bandmaster and composer, led a band of his own musicians.

As the end of the parade rolled past, thousands of spectators standing on the sidewalks joined in, and the parade began to lengthen and grow in size. It was the march of the umbrellas. Flutes played and bass drums boomed as thousands with their dark umbrellas marched to the music.

When the parade entered Wall Street, the ticker tape, confetti, and other small papers began to fly from every window. It looked like a winter snowstorm with the air thick with white specks and streamers of paper. The paper blanketed everything: tubas and rifles and the ears of the horses.

It was time for Philippe and his father to make their move to the South Street docks to board the steamboat to Bedloe's Island. During the time they had worked on the statue, they took a smaller boat and were used to the trip, but today more than three hundred boats were steaming to the island.

Men in tall black silk hats carried picnic box lunches and picnic baskets. Women in gray cloaks carried colored umbrellas with tasseled fringes. Children of all sizes, workers dressed in the clothes of their trade, souvenir peddlers, and even pickpockets — all clamored to board the boats.

"All aboard for the *Magnolia!*"

"Ticket holders for the *Grand Republic*, board here!"

More than three hundred boats of every description awaited passengers. Some were so large they could hold three thousand, while others could barely contain one family. Blasts of steam from whistles pierced the air. Water from the paddle wheelers churned. Toots and pips, honks, and low warbles — all from the boats — sounded like a band tuning up. The parade on land seemed quiet and organized compared with the confusion at the docks.

Philippe and his father were squashed between a railing and

three French journalists. There was absolutely no place to move, but at least they were aboard.

Furiously, the boats left the docks in a huge *whoosh*. They raced into the Hudson River around the tip of New York and formed two lines through which President Cleveland's ship, the S.S. *Tennessee,* would pass. Despite the cold, damp afternoon, champagne bubbled over as passengers fired corks from one boat to another.

*M*ore than 300 boats of all kinds took part in the sea parade. Here the Presidential launch approaches Bedloe's Island.

At 2:30 P.M. the *Tennessee* left her dock and fired her cannons, which signaled the start of the naval review. The noise grew to a deafening pitch as every boat saluted the presidential warship with whistles and cannon fire. By 3:00 P.M., President Cleveland arrived aboard a launch at Bedloe's Island where a twenty-one gun salute welcomed him. Other important guests arrived and took their seats near the base of the statue.

Near the dock at Bedloe's Island, Bartholdi came running over to Philippe.

"I have been looking all over for you," Bartholdi said. "Where have you been?"

"We just arrived. The boat could not dock because there were so many other boats unloading passengers," explained Philippe.

"Good afternoon, Monsieur Peden. You look splendid in your new suit," said Bartholdi.

"Sir," M. Peden said, in some pain, "I have helped you build a statue and *you* have been the downfall of my feet!"

"Come now, when you sit down with the others, you can loosen your shoes," said Bartholdi to M. Peden sympathetically. "As for you, Philippe, you will come with me. You see that boy over there, he will give us the signal after Senator Evarts finishes his speech. He will wave a white handkerchief. We will be in the torch, so we will not be able to hear the speeches through all the noise, music, and cannon fire." Bartholdi waved to the signal boy and the boy waved back.

Then Philippe and the sculptor raced up the stairs of the pedestal to the first level, where the pedestal meets the statue. Bartholdi paused to take a breath. "Let's take it slower," Bartholdi suggested. "I am not as young as you are, Philippe." The sounds of their footsteps on the iron stairs echoed through the hollow body of the statue. Up ahead they saw light. "It must be the windows of the crown," Philippe thought to himself.

Finally they arrived at the crown level. Bartholdi, quite out of breath, slowly walked over to one of the windows, took some raindrops from the window sill and patted them on his face. He reached out and pulled aside a corner of the flag that was in front of the Liberty's face. The view was magnificent!

"Look at this, Philippe! Thousands of ships, small and large, two thousand people on Bedloe's Island, the President of the United States, New York City, the friendship of two great nations, and a statue that has finally reached her full size. She is ready to be born. We have done all we can. Now we must unveil her so her face will enlighten the world." Bartholdi grinned from ear to ear. He had toiled for twenty-one years and now the moment had come: years into minutes. He turned to Philippe and said, "Lead on, young man."

The door to the torch swung open, and the sculptor and Philippe climbed the steep rungs of the ladder-like stairs. Then, through a small door, they emerged into the salty, misty, rain-soaked air. From where they stood in the torch, they could feel the excitement mounting, though they could not see much through the fog.

The first speaker, Dr. Richard Storrs, a minister, offered a simple prayer that was interrupted at once by a tugboat whistle. Then Count de Lesseps, the head of the French delegation, spoke in French.

"The old man is really in top form," Bartholdi said, leaning over the railing of the torch as he watched the gray haired Count de Lesseps wave his arms and speak. "I can't hear most of the words, but I can hear the audience applaud. They seem to like him, even though they cannot understand what he is saying."

"Monsieur Bartholdi, please explain to me how I can assist

you in unveiling Liberty's face from under the tricolor flag," said Philippe.

"When the time comes, the boy will wave his handkerchief and you will tell me he has given the signal. Then I will pull this rope, which is now tied to the railing of the torch. The flag will be released and float to the ground."

"But the flag is so wet. It will not float, it will drop like a wet chicken," said Philippe.

"Philippe, a man can do everything in his power to create something that will be perfect. It has taken me twenty-one years of my life to get to this spot atop this torch, holding this rope. Certainly, the day would have been better if the sun had come out. But that really doesn't matter. What does matter is that we are here and we are making history; history is not making us. That is the sign of greatness in a man. That you leave your mark where *you* want."

Count de Lesseps had finished speaking and now Senator Evarts was to begin. For a brief moment, perhaps a second or two, the thick clouds cleared a little, letting a few rays of sunlight through. "It is a good sign," thought Philippe. But then the clouds rolled in again.

Senator Evarts began speaking in his slow voice. His first sentences were so complicated, they seemed to take forever. After a time, he stopped for a breath before he continued. But to the signal boy, it seemed as if he had finished! "He is waving his handkerchief," shouted Philippe.

"No, no, that is impossible. It is too soon. This speaker is very long winded!" argued Bartholdi.

"No, monsieur. He is waving it. It is the signal, there is no mistake," Philippe said loudly.

Bartholdi grabbed the rope in his rain-soaked hands. His arms shivered with goose bumps. "Now," he muttered to himself. He tugged the rope. The clips holding the flag opened and the flag dropped away from the face of the

"No, monsieur. He is waving it. It is the signal, there is no mistake," Philippe said loudly.

Statue. The senator resumed his speech as the flag fell. But suddenly a deafening cheer was heard. Whistles and horns from the boats anchored off Bedloe's Island resounded. Cannons were fired from Manhattan, Staten Island, Brooklyn, and New Jersey. Everyone assembled at the base of the statue rose and threw their silk top hats up into the damp air. The noise echoed across the bay, growing louder and more intense, like rolling thunder. Church bells pealed at the same time from all the neighboring cities.

In the torch, high above, Philippe and Bartholdi danced around the copper flame like dizzy moths. They were jubilant.

The only person who could not understand what had happened was Senator Evarts. He had not yet realized that the Liberty had been unveiled. He turned around and saw the face of the statue. Evarts blushed and sat down.

The band on the island played "America." And for nearly twenty minutes, the shouting and celebrating continued wildly.

"Oh, to be alive in these times," thought Philippe. He turned to M. Bartholdi and said, "Just as Liberty has changed your life, so has it changed mine. Paris, America, New York...I pledge to you on this torch that I shall keep this statue in my heart for the rest of my life." Bartholdi embraced Philippe.

Below, President Cleveland took the speaker's platform. In a loud voice he proclaimed, "We will not forget that Liberty has here made her home, nor shall her chosen altar be neglected." And the applause rose again.

Philippe and Bartholdi descended. Slowly and softly they walked down the spiral staircase. As they reached the open air, they walked into a sea of journalists and were picked up and carried aloft by the crowd.

CHAPTER EIGHT

REMEMBERING LIBERTY

"**C**an you see it, Claude?"

"Yes, there it is, Nelly. With a huge ship passing it. It is the S.S. *Normandie.* You can tell by the French flag. Look at that, Grand-papa! Fantastique!!"

"Grand-papa says that when you get closer, from the deck of a ship, that is when the statue really looks her best, as if she is about to walk off her pedestal and right across the harbor."

"I can't wait to go up into her head. I am going to walk up all 167 steps."

Philippe Peden stood on the observation deck of the world's tallest building, the Empire State Building, looking across the rooftops of New York City to the world's tallest statue. Philippe was no longer a child as he was when he saw the model of the statue for the first time. He was now a man of sixty-six. In fact, he was a grandfather to Claude, aged ten, and Nelly, aged eight.

It was 1937. Philippe was in New York to work but also to celebrate. The statue had just had her fiftieth birthday. Through the years, Philippe had become quite famous as a coppersmith. He had specialized in statues and was known as *the* greatest master coppersmith in all of France. So it was only natural that when the statue needed to be repaired, Philippe was asked to help with the work. But Philippe Peden didn't consider it work, it was far more than that. Ever since the time he had been an apprentice, the Statue of Liberty had been a personal symbol in his life.

"Claude, you see the way the sun's rays touch the statue. You know, it looks different at each hour of the day. And, Nelly look how all the ships entering the harbor pass the Liberty on her left. It certainly is a grand sight!"

"Was the statue always green, Grand-papa?" asked Nelly, looking through the observation deck binoculars of the Empire State Building.

"No, Nelly," her brother interrupted. "It is made of copper. And when copper is left outside, it turns green. Especially when it is exposed to the sun, wind, and sea air."

"Exactly so," added Philippe, patting his grandson on the head. "Let's sit on the bench over there. I want to tell you some things about the statue that you probably don't know."

The three of them walked over to the bench and sat down, the children sitting on either side of their grandfather. Philippe fished in his pocket and pulled out something in his hand. He put his two hands behind his back and brought them out in front of him. "Guess which hand?" he asked playfully.

"Left," said Nelly tapping the left hand.

"No, right," said Claude.

"You are both..." Philippe opened his two hands, "correct. Do you know what that is?" he asked.

"Copper," both children chimed at the same time.

"There is an interesting story about this copper. It was given to me when I was eleven years old by Frédéric Auguste Bartholdi, the sculptor of the Statue of Liberty. See, on it is written 'Fragment de cuivre de la Statue Colossal de la Liberté executée par A. Bartholdi (*A piece of copper from the colossal Statue of Liberty built by A. Bartholdi.*)' M. Bartholdi gave me these small pieces of the actual copper used on the statue. I have saved these carefully, knowing that someday, when the moment was right, I would give them to the two children I love most in the world."

Philippe handed Claude and Nelly each one of the rare copper souvenirs.

"It is a more beautiful color than the green the statue has become," observed Claude, examining the copper.

"I think the green is also pretty. It matches the sky and water," said Nelly, holding the copper in the sunlight.

"No, the real copper is nicer," Claude insisted.

"Don't argue, children. Both are beautiful. That is the special quality of copper. It is golden when it is new and it turns green as the trees and the grass when it ages. M. Bartholdi told me that. *My* father told me that. And I, who have worked with copper for fifty years, know it to be true."

"It's so thin, like an American silver dollar. How can it stand there in the harbor for so many years without falling down?" asked Nelly.

"You're right, Nelly. It is very thin. On its own, the copper could not stand alone. But when we built the statue, M. Bartholdi asked his friend Gustave Eiffel, the same man who built the Eiffel Tower, to design an iron skeleton for it. It is the iron skeleton that holds it up. The copper is only the outer shape and skin of the statue," explained Philippe.

"Just like real people! We have bones. And we have skin," added Claude.

"Only mine is not green," added Nelly sadly.

Philippe and Claude laughed.

"Children, you must make me a promise never to sell these

"Why are there tears in your eyes, Grand-papa?" asked Claude, concerned about his grandfather.

pieces of Liberty. Save them for your children and their children — people you love and care about," added Philippe quietly.

"Why are there tears in your eyes, Grand-papa?" asked Claude, concerned about his grandfather.

"Oh, it's nothing," Philippe said, sniffing and wiping the tears with a handkerchief. "I guess I am very happy. Sometimes adults cry when they are happy. These copper pieces have been in my top pocket, near my heart, for a long time. They have brought me good luck in life. I am crying because I am happy to be able to give them to you. Anyway," he said, changing the mood, "they were very heavy after so many years of carrying them around. Your grandmother would always say, 'Philippe, you will lose those copper pieces because they are putting holes in your pockets.' And you know, she was right." Philippe pulled out his right coat pocket — there was a hole in it. Then his left coat pocket — another hole. And his pants pockets — more holes. Nelly and Claude started to laugh.

"Liberty holes, Liberty holes," she sang. And the three of them laughed so hard they soon were all in tears.

"Nelly, Claude — as you know, your Grand-papa loves the statue almost as much as he loves you. It seems that through my life our paths — Liberty's and mine — keep crossing. How would you like to know more about her?" asked Philippe.

"Yes, yes, that would be great," cheered Nelly.

"Can we visit her?" asked Claude hopefully.

"I don't see why not. I already have the boat tickets. Here they are," Philippe said, waving three tickets.

"Fantastique!" cried the children, jumping up and down.

By the time they arrived at the dock at the very tip of Manhattan, it was already 1:00 P.M. The sky was a deep blue, and the clouds on this September day were like long thin loaves of bread.

"Those clouds remind me of lunch," said Claude licking his lips.

"Oh, everything reminds you of food," said Nelly, poking her brother in his stomach.

"We'll buy something to eat on Bedloe's Island when we arrive," offered Philippe.

Just then the small double-decker ferryboat tooted its whistle as it pulled into the ferry slip. The passengers walked down the gangway and onto shore. Small children, men, women, teenagers, even babies being carried by grandmothers, came ashore. Some held little models of the statue made of white metal, others held flags and pennants in the shape of a long triangle. It felt more like going to the circus than a trip to the biggest statue in the world.

"All aboard for the Statue of Liberty!" cried the deckhand.

"Quickly, children, up the steps, up the steps," called Philippe. And then there was a big push and, in a moment, the wooden ferryboat was filled up and the captain blew his whistle. The water churned, passengers babbled, and seagulls flew overhead in wide circles, as the ferry started its short run across New York harbor.

"Oh Grand-papa, this is exciting. My heart is pounding," cried Nelly breathlessly.

"My stomach's growling," complained Claude.

"He's always hungry," said Nelly to her grandfather.

"It was a view like this that millions of hungry immigrants saw when they arrived in America. You see that island over there," Philippe said, pointing to a large red brick building. "That is Ellis Island, where since 1892 more than twenty million new immigrants have landed when they came to

America — right past the Statue of Liberty. During the last war the Statue of Liberty was used as a symbol by the Americans to help raise money for the war effort. It was the first time she was used as an official symbol for the whole country."

"Grand-papa, what exactly is a symbol?" asked Nelly.

"I know," Claude said quickly. "A symbol stands for another thing. Like the tricolor flag stands for France," he continued.

"That's true," Philippe agreed. "Symbols remind us of ideas, but they are not the ideas themselves."

"Oh, so the statue reminds us of liberty and freedom, but it, itself, is not really liberty and is not really freedom," explained Nelly.

"That's very good, Nelly," said Philippe. "When the new immigrants arrived in America, the first view they had from the ship was New York harbor and the statue. The statue reminded them that in this new country, they would have the liberty to do many things which they could not do in their old countries. In a few minutes we shall arrive, children," Philippe added.

"From here Grand-papa, she is a giant. Not only the statue but the pedestal that she is standing on," announced Claude, impressed by his first close-up sight of Miss Liberty.

"Believe it or not, when I was about fifteen years old, I worked way up there," Philippe proudly stated as he pointed to the torch and crown. "With *my* father. It was a great honor. I was even here on Bedloe's Island when they unveiled the statue on October 28, 1886. And this year, when the statue was fixed up for her fiftieth birthday, I worked on *top* of her head, fixing the rays of her crown. You see, here is a picture." And Philippe showed Nelly and Claude a photograph.

Philippe, the two children, and the rest of the boatload of

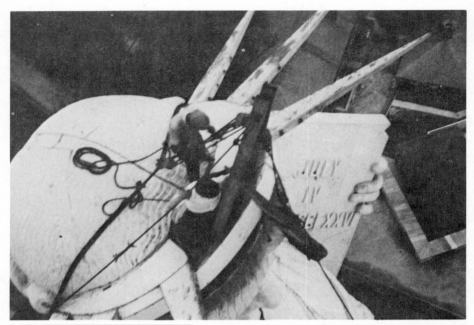

*I*n 1937 repairs were made on the spikes of the crown.

*I*n 1886, workers were busy to the last minute finishing the interior of Liberty's head.

passengers walked down the long wooden dock onto Bedloe's Island. As they walked, staring up at the statue, the
crowd thinned out.

"Let's wait until the others go up," suggested Philippe. "It is
best to first feel the size of the statue from the outside.
People often make that mistake and race inside immediately
to see the view. But then they miss the Liberty herself. You
see, the statue was built in the center of an old military fort
— Fort Wood. The pedestal rises almost nine stories above
ground and reaches down several stories below ground."

From the walkway around the island, the view of New York
harbor, with its ships and bridges, was spectacular....
"When we put the statue together out here during the
spring and summer of '86, there used to be a small railway
on the island — not one with a steam engine, just horse-
drawn wagons that would help the men pull the heavy crates
from the dock to this area," Philippe said, pointing to a

*A*n aerial view of the statue and the walkway around the island.

grassy spot. "Tourists loved to pose for photographs, sitting near different parts of the statue." Philippe and the children sat down on the grass. "I ate many workman's lunches, sitting out here on this part of the island. There was this Italian boy, a new immigrant named Vincent. His father was a stonemason and Vincent was an apprentice to his father, just as I was an apprentice to mine. We became friends right here on this island. After lunch we used to walk to the water's edge and skip flat stones. We thought maybe the stones would reach the new East River Bridge, three miles away. I wonder whatever happened to Vincent? For a couple of months, he was the closest friend I had."

"Is your grandfather telling you all his Liberty stories?" Nelly and Claude turned around. Philippe kept looking at the bridge in the distance.

"Bill Farnham," said Philippe, without looking around. "I'd know that voice of yours anywhere. Nelly and Claude, this is the National Parks superintendent of the island. He's an old friend."

Claude and Nelly shook his hand. Farnham spoke to the children, "How would you kids like me to show you some secrets about the statue, because you're special visitors? But first, what I have to see is something made of copper," Bill Farnham said seriously (with a little smile).

Nelly and Claude dug in their pockets and pulled out the copper Philippe had given them. "My word," said Bill, winking at Philippe, "two original pieces of Liberty's copper. I thought you would each show me a penny. Well, you know what this means. You get to climb into the torch. The torch has been closed to visitors for years and years. But on special occasions, like this one, and for very important people, we make rare exceptions."

The four of them entered the base of the statue to take the elevator up to the top of the pedestal. From there, a winding stairway was the only way to get to the top. "Are you still hungry, Claude?" asked Philippe.

"No, Grand-papa. I forgot all about that. This is much more interesting than food. We'll eat later."

Nelly winked at Philippe, and Philippe smiled back at her.

As they rode to the top of the pedestal, the elevator operator, a National Parks guide, explained to them about Bartholdi and the whole history of the statue. He even told them how long her nose was (4 feet 6 inches), her eyes (2 feet), and her fingernails (13 inches across).

"Here we are," said Bill. "All out." And then, they walked up the circular stairs to the top — all 167 steps!

They entered the room where millions and millions before them had looked out on one of the greatest cities in the world. "This is a strange room. What are these wavy lines on the ceiling?" asked Nelly.

"Those lines form the hair of the statue. And this room is her head. Pretty big head, isn't it, Nelly? Let's take a look out," said Bill, pointing to the windows.

Nelly and Claude walked over to the windows that were part of the crown.

"Oh, Grand-papa. Look at the toy boats!" cried Nelly, standing on her tiptoes.

"They are real boats, silly. They only look tiny," Claude remarked impatiently.

Bill walked over to a small side door and unlocked it with a key he wore around his neck. "Nelly, Claude, now listen. I'll go first, and then you'll follow me, Claude. Then Nelly, and then you'll be last, Philippe. Children, hold onto the railing tightly and, whatever you do, don't look down," Bill concluded as he began the climb into the arm.

They climbed up the steep, narrow stairs that were almost like a ladder. "Everyone all right?" Bill asked. And his voice echoed in the tunnel-like arm.

"This is scary," said Nelly, in a frightened voice.

"You're fine, Nelly, I am right behind you," said Philippe, in a calming voice. "Only a few more steps."

Suddenly there was strange amber light and then they entered the torch just below the flame. "What are these windows for?" asked Claude.

"What huge light bulbs!" said Nelly.

Bill opened the small door to the outside of the torch. The fresh air felt good after they had been in the hot, humid arm of the statue. Ah, what a breeze.

Once up, Nelly held Philippe's hand, and Claude held Bill's hand.

"Fantastique!" yelled Claude, shouting into the sky.

"Grand-papa, I don't like being up here with the birds. This isn't a place for people. It makes me dizzy," Nelly said in a frail, timid voice.

"This torch is not exactly the original," explained Bill. "It was redesigned in 1916. The original had a solid copper surface. And then in 1887, one year after the Liberty went up, some lights were added on the outside of the statue, just under the flame of the torch. But the lights blinded thousands of birds, which were killed when they flew into them."

"Like moths around a candle," said Claude.

"Poor birds," said Nelly sadly.

"Then in 1916, pieces of the torch were cut out and replaced with panes of red and yellow glass, the kind they use in churches. Lights were added. And finally the torch was lit brightly and beautifully. Sailors at sea could pinpoint New York harbor at night because the torch had really become a beacon." Bill knew the history of the statue like the back of his hand. Like Philippe, he shared a deep feeling for this extraordinary piece of art that was bigger than most buildings.

Thousands of birds were blinded by the new lighting system of 1887.

Below them, sea gulls and terns glided on the rising air currents and sea wind. The sun glinted off the copper railing and reflected in the glass of the torch. Tugboats were pushing a large ocean liner from the bay into the open sea. Their foamy wakes trailed behind them in straight lines and twinkled in the late afternoon sun.

115

"Grand-papa, this is the best day I have ever had. I am very lucky to have a grandfather who helped build the statue," exclaimed Nelly.

"You can read the book Liberty is holding," Claude said, leaning over the railing.

"Hold on to my hand tightly, Claude," warned Bill.

They carefully walked down the steep steps of the arm, into the head of the statue again. They walked down the iron spiral stairs in the middle of the statue's body. What an eerie feeling, corkscrewing down and around and around. "Take that door to the right, kids," Bill pointed out. Once again, as they walked through the door, they were out in the air; only now they were on the top promenade of the pedestal.

"You can see all the complicated folds in her robes," said Philippe. "I remember how long those took to make. Nearly three hundred different pieces, all to be fit together."

"Just like a puzzle," suggested Claude.

"Who would like some ice cream?" asked Bill, checking his watch.

Nelly and Claude raised their hands and jumped up and down.

"Chocolate," said Nelly.

"Vanilla," said Claude.

At the base of the pedestal they sat near the refreshment stand, enjoying the last part of the afternoon, until the ferryboat arrived with a few last-minute sightseers. Many passengers had lined up to take the boat back. All day long, every week, for years and years, a steady stream of people from all over the world made a journey to this symbol of liberty. In this respect she was the eighth wonder of the world.

"Bill, I never thought in my wildest dreams that I would see

A torch, a book, and a crown. All together, the Statue of Liberty — The Statue
in the Harbor.

the day when I would take my grandchildren to the very Statue of Liberty I took part in constructing when I was a young apprentice. You can't imagine the feeling of satisfaction. It is like showing off your favorite thing to your favorite friends," said Philippe emotionally.

"I know just how you feel, Philippe. I see her every day, and yet she means something new to me each time, like a living idea. One day they should really change the name of Bedloe's Island to Liberty Island," suggested Bill.

"They will. They will," assured Philippe.

Nelly and Claude finished their ice cream and thanked Bill for his expert tour. "Hey kids," called Bill, "how about a souvenir of your visit?"

"We have our grandfather," answered Claude. "He is the best souvenir we could have."

The ferryboat tooted, the water churned under the decks, and Philippe and his two grandchildren gazed back at the statue. She was silhouetted by the setting sun, which was almost directly behind her torch and head. The torch caught a ray of reddish sunlight, making the uplifted hand glow. Nelly had fallen asleep. In her hand she clutched a piece of copper from the statue in the harbor.

APPENDIX 1

THE NEW COLOSSUS

In the autumn of 1883, the American Pedestal Committee, in its effort to raise funds for the construction on Bedloe's Island, called on well-known American writers and artists to donate an original sample of their work for an exhibition-sale. Mark Twain and William Dean Howells sent in manuscripts as did a young poet named Emma Lazarus.

At first Emma Lazarus told the Committee that she didn't think she could write something about the statue. But then an idea came to her: more than anything else the statue would welcome new immigrants arriving from Europe. Lazarus called the statue a "Mother of Exiles." Little did she know that this name would describe the statue in years to come.

Emma Lazarus's poem was well received in 1883. But it was not until 1904, when the poem was placed on a bronze plaque inside the statue, that the meaning of the poem became clear. In her own way, Emma Lazarus became the prophet of Liberty. Today her words are as well known as the statue itself.

THE NEW COLOSSUS

Not like the brazen giant of Greek fame,
With conquering limbs astride from land to land;
Here at our sea-washed, sunset gates shall stand
A mighty woman with a torch, whose flame
Is the imprisoned lightning, and her name
Mother of Exiles. From her beacon-hand
Glows world-wide welcome; her mild eyes command
The air-bridged harbor that twin cities frame.
"Keep ancient lands, your storied pomp!" cries she
With silent lips. "Give me your tired, your poor,
Your huddled masses yearning to breathe free,
The wretched refuse of your teeming shore.
Send these, the homeless, tempest-tost to me,
I lift my lamp beside the golden door!"

EMMA LAZARUS

APPENDIX 2

THE CENTENNIAL RESTORATION OF THE
STATUE OF LIBERTY
1886–1986

For more than 36,000 days and nights the Statue of Liberty has stood in New York harbor. Through rain and snow, winds and sun she has braved the elements. In 1916, a nearby explosion popped out some of her rivets. Her original torch was replaced with a new one. She has received numerous coats of paint on the inside of her copper body. Long ago her bright, copper-colored skin turned a shade of bottle green from exposure to the sea air. Through the years the statue has been repaired as needed, and in 1936, when she was fifty, she was given her first face-lift.

Now, for the statue's centennial in 1986, workers are once again busy repairing and cleaning the statue. New stairways and elevators are being installed. Old paint is being removed. The iron straps and bracing that Gustave Eiffel designed are being replaced with stainless steel materials. A new lighting system will brighten her overall appearance. Engineers and workers are strengthening her rivets.

The torch, which has served for so many years as a beacon of freedom, is being completely rebuilt according to Bartholdi's original plan. French coppersmiths have been invited to construct its flame. This new flame will duplicate the original except that this time it will be gilded with gold. Bartholdi himself would have approved of the careful attention which has been paid to all the details.

When the work is completed in 1986, the Statue of Liberty will be rededicated. The torch will be relit. America and France and the rest of the world will celebrate the statue's centennial in the grand fashion of the original dedication of 100 years ago.

...And American Liberty will once again enlighten the world!

APPENDIX 3

DIMENSIONS OF THE STATUE

	Feet	Inches
Height from base to torch	151	1
Foundation of pedestal to torch	305	1
Heel to top of head	111	1
Length of hand	16	5
Index finger	8	0
Circumference at second joint	3	6
Size of fingernail, 13 × 10 inches		
Head from chin to cranium	17	3
Head thickness from ear to ear	10	0
Distance across the eye	2	6
Length of nose	4	6
Right arm, length	42	0
Right arm, greatest thickness	12	0
Thickness of waist	35	0
Width of mouth	3	0
Tablet, length	23	7
Tablet, width	13	7
Tablet, thickness	2	0
Height of granite pedestal	89	0
Height of foundation	65	0

Weight of copper used in statue, 200,000 pounds (100 tons).
Weight of steel used in statue, 250,000 pounds (125 tons).
Total weight of statue, 450,000 pounds (225 tons).
Copper sheeting of statue is 3/32-inch thick.

SELECTED FURTHER READING

Bartholdi and the Statue of Liberty. Willadene Price. Skokie, Ill.: Rand McNally & Co., 1959.

I Lift My Lamp: The Way of the Symbol. Hertha Pauli and E.B. Ashton. Originally published by Appleton-Century-Crofts, 1948; republished by Empire State Historical Publications, 1969.

Meet Miss Liberty. Lillie Patterson. New York: Macmillan Publishing Co., 1962.

Statue of Liberty. Oscar Handlin. New York: Newsweek Books, 1971.

Statue of Liberty. Marvin Trachtenberg. New York: Viking Penguin, Inc., 1976.

The Statue of Liberty Enlightening the World. Frédéric Auguste Bartholdi. Originally published in 1885; republished with new introduction by Jeffrey Eger. New York: New York Bound, Inc., 1984.

Statue of Liberty: Heritage of America. Paul Weinbaum. Gweneth R. DenDooven, ed. Las Vegas, Nev.: KC Publications, 1980.

The Statue of Liberty in Postcards. Jeffrey Eger, ed. Mineola, N.Y.: Dover Publications, Inc., 1985.